SANTA'S BABY

COMING HOME FOR CHRISTMAS

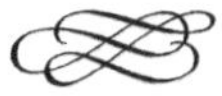

SYLVIA MCDANIEL

Coming Home for Christmas

I'll Be Home for Christmas
White Christmas
Santa's Baby
All I Want For Christmas
Box Set

Mistletoe and a Secret Baby: Rekindling Love in the Season of Miracles

Nine months ago amid the sun-kissed waves of a cruise, Amelia Miller and Ryan Allen share a magical night that neither can forget. The spark between them is instant, the connection undeniable. But when the ship docks, they are separated before sharing last names.

Now, on the cusp of the holiday season, fate throws them an unexpected curveball. Ryan and his fellow EMTs receive an urgent call to a hotel where a pregnant woman is in labor. To his astonishment, he finds the mother-to-be is none other than Amelia carrying a precious secret: their child.

In this heartwarming, contemporary holiday romance, old flames are rekindled as Ryan and Amelia are brought together by the impending arrival of their baby. Among the joy, challenges, and the secret that binds them, can they create a future filled with the warmth of a second chance at love? Join them in this unforgettable tale of insta-love, secret babies, and the magic of the holiday season.

CHAPTER 1

*A*pril

Tonight was the last night of the cruise, and Amelia Miller intended to make it count.

The bass thundered through the main lounge, vibrating up through the soles of her heels and into her chest. Colored lights swept across the dance floor in time with the music, painting the crowd in shades of electric blue and magenta. She'd been dancing for hours, and her skin hummed with exertion and champagne and the intoxicating freedom of knowing that, for the first time in two years, she had nothing to prove.

The bar exam was behind her. Passed. The job offer from Morrison & Clarke in Cheyenne was signed and sealed. Monday morning, she would walk into that prestigious law firm as Attorney Amelia Miller, but tonight, tonight she was just a woman who wanted to dance until her feet gave out.

Taylor grabbed her hand and spun her around, both of them laughing, breathless. They'd been friends since their first brutal week of law school, bonded by stress, too much coffee, and the shared determination to make it through. Taylor had kept her sane through the worst of it, and when Amelia's parents had gifted her this cruise as a congratulations present, there had been no question who she'd bring along.

"I need a break," Taylor shouted over the music, fanning herself. "And another drink."

Amelia nodded, following her friend back to their table near the edge of the dance floor. She sank into her chair, grateful for the moment to catch her breath. The DJ transitioned into another song, something with a Latin beat that made her want to get right back up.

That's when she saw him again.

He stood near the bar, and even in the shifting lights, she could see he was watching her. They'd been playing this game all week, stolen glances across the pool deck, lingering looks at dinner, that one moment in the elevator when their eyes had met and held for three floors before the doors opened and the spell broke. She'd wondered each time if he would approach, if she would, but neither of them had made the move.

Until now.

He was cutting through the crowd, headed straight for their table, and Amelia's heart kicked up a rhythm that had nothing to do with dancing. Even in the dim light, she could see the confident set of his shoulders, the easy way he moved. Tall, dark hair that looked like he'd run his hands through it a few times, and those eyes. Even from a distance, she'd noticed those eyes, bright green and impossibly expressive.

He stopped at their table, and up close, he was even more devastating than she'd allowed herself to admit. A white button-down shirt with the sleeves rolled to his forearms, dark jeans that fit him perfectly, and a smile that made something low in her belly tighten with want.

"Would you dance with me?" he asked.

His voice was smooth, with just a hint of gravel that made it interesting. Amelia felt Taylor kick her under the table, a clear message to say yes, you idiot, but she was already nodding, already reaching for his extended hand.

"Of course."

His palm was warm against hers as he led her onto the dance floor. The song shifted, and she recognized the opening bars of a Texas two-step. Before she could worry about keeping up, he pulled her into position, and they were moving.

Oh, he was good. Really good. He led with confidence but not arrogance, spinning her out and reeling her back in with perfect timing. Amelia had taken dance lessons in college, a requirement for some sorority formal she'd long forgotten, but she'd never had a partner who made it feel this effortless, this fun. His hand at the small of her back was firm and sure, guiding her through turns she didn't know she could make.

When he pulled her close for an underarm turn, she

caught his scent, something clean and masculine with a hint of cedar and spice. It made her want to lean in closer, to press her face against his neck and breathe him in. The thought sent a flush of heat through her that had nothing to do with the exertion of dancing.

The song ended too soon, and they walked off the floor together, his hand still at her back. The contact felt natural, right, like they'd done this a hundred times before.

"You're an excellent dancer," she said, slightly breathless.

"Thank you." His smile was genuine, pleased. "Can I buy you a drink?"

"Please."

She returned to the table while he headed to the bar. Taylor was nowhere in sight, probably out on the dance floor with the guy she'd been flirting with earlier. Just as well. Amelia wanted this man to herself.

He returned with two drinks, something colorful with a tiny umbrella, and slid into the seat beside her. Close enough that their knees touched under the table, and neither of them moved away.

"You've been watching me all week," Amelia said, deciding to be direct. She was tired of games, of waiting. "I kept expecting you to come over."

He had the grace to look slightly embarrassed, his smile turning sheepish. "I know. I'm attracted to you, obviously, but I had to work up my courage. You're..." He gestured at her, as if that explained everything. "Beautiful doesn't quite cover it."

Amelia felt herself flush with pleasure. She wasn't

fishing for compliments, but hearing it said so plainly, so honestly, made her chest warm. "What's your name?"

"Ryan." He picked up her hand from where it rested on the table, his thumb brushing over her knuckles. The simple touch sent sparks up her arm. "And you are?"

"Amelia."

"Amelia," he repeated, like he was testing how it sounded. She liked the way it rolled off his tongue. "Want to dance again?"

She was already standing, pulling him toward the floor. This time, the DJ was playing something slow and sultry, all bass and yearning vocals. Ryan didn't hesitate, he pulled her against him, one hand at her waist, the other finding hers. Amelia let her free hand rest on his shoulder, then slide up to the back of his neck, her fingers brushing the soft hair there.

This close, she could feel the solid warmth of him, the lean muscle beneath his shirt. He smelled even better up close, and when he tucked her tighter against his body, she felt the evidence of his attraction pressing against her hip. The knowledge that he wanted her sent a thrill through her that she hadn't felt in years.

For over two years, she'd done nothing but study. No dating, no distractions, nothing but constitutional law, torts, and civil procedure. She'd promised herself that once the bar exam was behind her, once she had that job offer in hand, she would let herself live again. Tonight felt like the permission she'd been waiting for.

When the song ended, Ryan didn't let her go immediately. Instead, he leaned down, his lips close to her ear. "Want to get out of here? Maybe walk the deck? It's quieter out there. We could actually talk."

Talk wasn't exactly what Amelia had in mind, but she nodded anyway. "Let me tell my friend."

She found Taylor at their table, and leaned down to whisper in her ear. "I'm going. See you in the morning."

Taylor grabbed her wrist. "Do you have your phone?"

"Yes, Mom," Amelia said with a grin.

"Be careful," Taylor said, glancing at Ryan with approval. "But have fun."

Oh, Amelia intended to.

She took Ryan's hand and let him lead her out of the club. The moment they stepped through the doors, the pounding music faded to a distant thump, replaced by the rush of wind and water. The night air was warm and slightly humid, carrying the salt-sweet smell of the ocean. Above them, stars scattered across the sky like diamonds on black velvet.

They walked toward the bow in comfortable silence, and Amelia found herself hyper-aware of everything, the way their hands fit together, the sound of their footsteps on the deck, the way the ship cut through the dark water below.

"I'm sad tonight's the last night," she said, looking out at the horizon. "I wish you'd come over sooner."

Ryan pulled her closer, turning so they faced each other. The moonlight caught his face, highlighting the sharp line of his jaw, the curve of his lips. "You're the first woman I've been interested in for a long time. It took me a while to work up the nerve."

"Divorced?" Amelia guessed.

"No." He didn't elaborate, and she didn't push. Tonight wasn't about histories or complications. "What about you? Why is someone like you on this cruise without a man?"

"I'm celebrating," she said, surprised by how much she wanted to share with him. "I spent two years doing nothing but studying for the bar exam. I finally passed last month, and I start at a law firm in Cheyenne on Monday. My parents gave me this cruise so I could decompress before real life starts."

"Congratulations." The word was simple, but the warmth in his voice made it feel significant. "That's impressive."

"Thank you." She tilted her head, studying him in the moonlight. "So what about you? Why is a handsome man like you cruising alone?"

"Needed a break from work," he said with a shrug. "Sometimes you have to step away from everything to remember who you are."

Before she could respond, he cupped her face in his hands and kissed her.

The world narrowed to the press of his lips on hers, warm and sure. He started gentle, almost questioning, but when Amelia made a soft sound of approval and opened to him, the kiss deepened. His tongue swept into her mouth, and she gripped his shoulders, suddenly dizzy with want.

Heat flooded through her, pooling low in her belly, and she pressed closer, needing more.

When they finally broke apart, both breathing hard, Amelia could only stare at him.

"I haven't been kissed like that in years," she whispered.

Ryan's laugh was low and rough. "I haven't given a kiss like that in years."

Amelia made a decision. Life was short, and opportunities like this didn't come along often. She was tired of being careful, of always doing the responsible thing. Tonight, she wanted to be reckless.

"You're not married, right?" she asked, just to be sure.

"Single," he confirmed. "Very single."

"Good." She ran her hand down his chest, feeling the solid muscle beneath the fabric. "Because I think we should go back to your room."

Ryan's eyes darkened, his pupils blown wide with desire. "You sure?"

"Very sure." Amelia pulled him closer, letting him feel how much she meant it. "We're two single people on the last night of a cruise. Let's not waste it."

A slow smile spread across his face. "My cabin. I have a suite. No roommate."

"Perfect."

They practically ran to the elevators, both of them grinning like teenagers. In the elevator, Ryan backed her against the wall and kissed her again, his hands on her waist, his body pressing her into the cool metal. By the time they reached the Verandah Deck, Amelia was trembling with anticipation.

His suite was nicer than her cabin, a separate bedroom, a small sitting area, and a balcony that overlooked the dark ocean. But Amelia barely registered any of it. The moment Ryan locked the door behind them, the air between them shifted, crackling with tension.

She reached behind herself and slowly unzipped her dress, letting the fabric slide down her body and pool at her feet. She stood before him in just her black lace bra, matching panties, and heels, watching his face as he took her in.

"Damn, Amelia," he breathed, and then he was on her, his hands in her hair, his mouth claiming hers with a hunger that matched her own.

She fumbled with the buttons of his shirt, desperate to feel his skin against hers. When she finally pushed the fabric off his shoulders, she had to pause and appreciate the view. His chest was beautifully defined, all lean muscle and smooth skin that she immediately wanted to explore with her hands, her mouth, everything.

"Tell me you have protection," she said against his lips.

"Multiple condoms," he assured her, his voice rough with desire. "We're covered."

"Thank God." She reached behind her back and unhooked her bra, letting it fall away.

Ryan's gaze dropped to her breasts, and the raw want in his expression made her feel powerful, desired in a way she hadn't in too long. Before she could say anything else, he scooped her up and carried her to the bedroom, laying her down on the bed with surprising gentleness.

"I've been thinking about this all week," he said, his hands running up her thighs.

"Then stop thinking," Amelia said, reaching for him. "And start doing."

He grinned, that devastating smile that had first caught her attention. "Oh no. We're taking our time with this. I want to savor every second."

And he did.

CHAPTER 2

$\mathcal{A}$melia lifted her mouth to his and Ryan met her halfway, his breath catching as their lips connected. For three years, three long, empty years, he hadn't kissed a woman, and tonight her sweet mouth had him dying for more. The softness of her lips, the warmth of her breath mingling with his, the tentative way she pressed against him as if testing whether this was real, it all conspired to undo him completely.

Why had he waited so long to finally take a chance and make a move?

The answer sat heavy in his chest, a weight he'd carried for far too long. His heart had loved another. Sandy's memory had kept him frozen in place, unable to move forward, unable to imagine wanting anyone else.

But somewhere between boarding this ship and watching Amelia laugh at dinner three nights ago, something had shifted. He'd finally realized he had to move on. He had to let himself live again.

And yet even now, even as Amelia's fingers threaded through his hair and pulled him closer, he knew this was nothing more than one night of two people satisfying their desires and easing their loneliness. Two ships passing in the night, literally. Tomorrow they'd dock in Miami and return to their separate lives. He'd go back to Missoula, and she'd disappear to wherever she came from.

But tonight? Tonight was theirs.

He'd been shocked when she suggested they get naked. They'd been dancing on the upper deck, the ocean breeze cool against their flushed skin, and she'd leaned in close and whispered the invitation in his ear.

He'd been surprised when she'd stripped down to her underwear without hesitation, revealing a body that made his mouth go dry and his hands shake with want. Yet he was so damn glad she'd been bold enough to ask for what she wanted. It had been way too long. Too long since he'd felt a woman's skin against his. Too long since he'd allowed himself to feel anything but grief.

It was time for him to heal, and tonight he'd taken the first step. Time for his life to begin again. Time for him to take a chance on another woman, even if just for these fleeting hours before dawn.

Her mouth covered his again, moving over his lips with increasing urgency, seeking comfort in an age-old connection. And Ryan was more than happy to return her kiss, eager, God, so eager, to once again create a raging passion between them. His hands roamed her back, tracing the curve of her spine, memorizing the feel of her.

All week he'd stared at her across the dining room, drawn to her auburn hair and bright eyes, wanting her with an intensity that had caught him off guard. But he'd been afraid. Afraid of betraying Sandy's memory.

Afraid of feeling something again. Afraid of the inevitable pain that came with caring. He'd wasted a lot of valuable time wrestling with ghosts and guilt.

Already he'd watched her come once, her back arching off the bed as his fingers worked between her thighs, her cries of pleasure echoing in his ears. The sight had nearly undone him. But now he wanted more. He wanted to be inside her when they came together. For them both to experience that long-forgotten feeling of being desired. Of being wanted. Of being cherished, if only for one night.

Moving over the top of her, Ryan savored the feeling of Amelia's breasts crushed against his chest, soft and warm and perfect. The feel of his cock hard and snug against her center made him groan. He was eager, almost desperate, to push inside her, to lose himself in her heat.

"Hurry," she whispered, her voice breathy and urgent.

"No," he replied, though every fiber of his being screamed at him to give them both what they wanted. "We've got all night and I plan on being inside you more than once. But this first time has to be special."

A whimper came from her throat, a sound of frustrated desire that sent heat coursing through his veins. His hand reached down between them to massage her clit, his fingers stroking the sensitive nub with the practiced touch of a man who'd once known a woman's body intimately.

Yes, it had been a while, three years was an eternity, but making love was like falling off a cliff. You quickly remembered all the nuances of where to step before you were ready to jump. The terrain became familiar again under your feet, muscle memory taking over where conscious thought faltered.

He wouldn't compare it to riding a bicycle because it was so much more dramatic than simply not falling. Jumping off a cliff was more like the feeling of reaching that pinnacle together, that moment of freefall where nothing existed but sensation and surrender and the person in your arms.

Taking a deep breath, Ryan sighed against her neck, inhaling deeply.

Women smelled so good. There was a special aroma about them that drew a man in, something primal and intoxicating that bypassed rational thought entirely. Amelia's body smelled of passion and possibility. A passion that was quickly enveloping him, pulling him under like a riptide. Her scent mixed with the salt air coming through the open balcony door, and he thought he'd never smelled anything more perfect in his life.

Sliding over to his side, one hand continued to play with her clit while the other stroked her silky skin, exploring every curve and valley. The touch of her warm, naked flesh beneath his fingers was intoxicating in a way that no whiskey or wine could ever match. The feel of a woman was better than anything on this earth. Soft where he was hard. Yielding where he was unyielding. And it had been way too long since he'd allowed himself this fundamental pleasure.

She moaned, the sound low and needy, encouraging him to continue. Her hands reached down, fingers grasping for him, but he caught her wrists gently and guided them away. He refused to let her touch him yet. He was a man, not a teenager, and he would not be releasing in her hand like some inexperienced boy fumbling in the dark.

"Not yet, darling, but soon," he whispered as his lips trailed up to her mouth and he moved back over her, covering her body with his. "Let me take care of you first."

It was time. He could see from her expression, eyes dark and glazed, lips parted, cheeks flushed, that she was ready to come once again. And this time, he wanted to be inside her when they both reached for the stars. He wanted to feel her clench around him, wanted to watch her face as pleasure overtook her, wanted to surrender to the moment together.

He leaned over and kissed the tops of her breasts one last time, letting his tongue trail over her smooth skin, tasting salt and sweetness. Her breasts were beautiful, soft and silky, and her nipples were taut with desire. He circled one with his tongue, then drew it into his mouth, savoring her sharp intake of breath.

Oh, how he wanted to make her feel good. He wanted to scatter her thoughts until nothing remained but pure sensation. He wanted to envelop her in sensual pleasure until she forgot her own name. He longed to hear her scream his name in the throes of desire, to know that he'd given her something memorable, something worth carrying back to her regular life. No one had done that for him for so very long, and he suspected she needed this as much as he did. It was time for both of them to feel alive again.

All week he'd watched her, wanting to get her into his bed, knowing instinctively that this woman would fill that empty part of him that had been hollow for so long. And hoping desperately that he did the same for her. This was a big step for him, bigger than she could possibly know. The first woman after losing the love of your life felt monumental, like crossing a threshold from which there was no return.

Her sapphire eyes had darkened to navy with desire and her breathing was quick and heavy, her chest rising and falling rapidly beneath him.

"Ryan," she said, her voice urgent and pleading. "Please. I need you."

It was time. He'd made them both wait long enough, and he was beyond ready to take her, to finally give in to what they'd been dancing around all week. Sliding on top of her, positioning himself at her entrance, he pushed his penis inside her slowly, giving her body time to adjust to him. But she raised her hips impatiently and took him all the way in with one swift movement, her muscles gripping him tight.

"Jesus," he groaned, his eyes nearly rolling back in his head at the sensation. She was hot and wet and perfect.

"I'm not going to last long," she said, her voice strained. "You've driven me wild with passion, making me wait all week. Making me wait tonight."

A chuckle rumbled from his chest despite the almost painful pleasure of being inside her. "That's what makes it so good, sweetheart. The anticipation. The build-up."

"Damn you," she cried, but there was laughter in her voice mixed with desperation. "Please, I want you to fuck me hard."

And he gave her exactly what she wanted.

Rising above her, bracing himself on his forearms, he slammed into her over and over, each thrust deliberate and deep. He watched the passion dance in her gaze, watched her pupils dilate and her mouth fall open.

The desire rose inside him like a wave, building and building until he couldn't hold it back any longer.

"Are you ready?" he asked, groaning as he felt his control slipping. "Tell me you're close."

"Yes," she cried out, her fingers digging into his shoulders. "God, yes. Please."

The intensity of his emotions and the overwhelming pleasure she was giving him had him moving faster, harder. He wanted to take her to new heights of pleasure. He wanted to give her everything, this one night of perfection before reality returned.

"Amelia," he cried out loud as he stared into her desire-filled eyes, holding his gaze as the two of them both reached for the stars together.

Her inner muscles clenched him deeply, pulsing around him, and he knew she was coming. He felt her body ripple with pleasure, felt her nails rake down his back.

"Ryan!" she gasped, his name torn from her throat.

With a mighty final thrust, he ground into her one last time and let himself go, the orgasm crashing over him with the force of three years of pent-up loneliness and need. For several long minutes, they didn't move, both of them trembling and gasping for air. Then he carefully pulled out of her and rolled her to her side, spooning her against his chest.

They lay there together, catching their breaths, their hearts slowly returning to normal rhythm. His arm draped over her waist, holding her close, and he pressed a kiss to her shoulder.

This was his first one-night stand and yet he didn't want it to end. This was the first woman since Sandy, and already he wondered where this lady lived. What she did for work. Whether she was as lonely in her regular life as he was in his. Could this be more than just a shipboard romance? Or was he being foolish, reading too much into good chemistry and mutual need?

"Damn, you do like to draw things out," she said with a breathless laugh.

He grinned against her skin. "Did you enjoy it?"

"Oh, yes," she whispered, pressing back against him. "More than I can say."

"Good," he said, already feeling himself stirring again as her curves molded against him. "Because I'm ready to go again whenever you are."

A giggle came from her and she snuggled closer, her hand covering his where it rested on her stomach. "Ryan, that was the best sex I've ever experienced. You've got until six o'clock in the morning. And then like Cinderella, I'll turn into a pumpkin and disappear."

Six o'clock. That gave them roughly seven more hours. Seven hours to memorize every inch of her. Seven hours to forget the past and ignore the future. Seven hours to feel human again.

"Then we better not waste a single minute," he said, already planning how he'd coax her name and phone number out of her before dawn. Maybe this didn't have to end at sunrise. Maybe, just maybe, this could be the beginning of something neither of them had been looking for but both desperately needed.

But right now, all he could concentrate on was this woman in his bed. This woman who had somehow, miraculously, chased the shadows away.

CHAPTER 3

Ryan awoke to brilliant sunlight streaming through the balcony doors of his suite, the harsh brightness stabbing into his eyes like an accusation. For a moment, he lay there disoriented, his body pleasantly sore in ways he'd almost forgotten were possible. Then memory flooded back, Amelia, her skin warm against his, her laughter soft in the darkness, the way she'd whispered his name as they'd made love for the third time just before dawn.

He sat up abruptly and reached across the bed at the same time, his hand searching for her warmth.

Empty. The sheets were cold.

"Amelia?" he called out, his voice rough with sleep and rising panic. "Amelia!"

He threw off the covers and stumbled toward the bathroom, hoping, praying, she was just in the shower or maybe out on the balcony watching the Miami skyline as they'd docked. Maybe she'd gone to grab them coffee from the café down the hall. Maybe she'd just stepped out for a moment.

But the bathroom was dark and empty. The balcony vacant except for two abandoned wine glasses from the night before. The silence in the suite was absolute, oppressive, damning.

Amelia was gone.

"Damn it," he said, running his hands through his hair as the full weight of his stupidity crashed down on him. "Damn it, damn it, damn it!"

How could he have fallen asleep? She'd told him, six o'clock and she'd turn into a pumpkin. He'd laughed at the Cinderella reference, had pulled her close, and promised he wouldn't let her disappear. And then, exhausted and sated after hours of lovemaking, he'd drifted off with her nestled in his arms.

And she'd slipped away like smoke.

How could he find her? He couldn't let her leave the ship without getting her contact information. Without giving her his number. Without figuring out if what they'd shared could become something more than one perfect night.

Wherever she lived, they would make it work. He'd drive to Cheyenne every weekend if he had to. Hell, he'd move there if it meant having more nights like last night. Last night had been wonderful, no, more than wonderful. It had been transformative. For the first time since the accident, he'd felt genuinely alive. And he didn't want their time together to end on a note of such colossal failure.

He grabbed his pants from the floor where he'd discarded them the night before and yanked them on, not bothering with underwear. A shirt came next, the buttons misaligned in his haste. He rushed out of his cabin barefoot, his only thought to get to her before it was too late.

The hallway was chaos, families with luggage, couples arguing over which bag held whose medications, children weaving between adults with the reckless abandon of those who'd been cooped up too long. Ryan pushed through the crowd, earning annoyed looks and muttered complaints he didn't bother acknowledging.

He had to find her before she left the ship.

Racing toward the elevator bank, his heart hammered against his ribs. Her cabin was on the third floor, he remembered that much from the conversation they'd had around two in the morning, both of them wrapped in sheets, sharing stories. She'd mentioned her room was smaller than his, had joked about splurging on the suite being worth it for the space alone.

The cruise was over, and he suddenly remembered his own disembarkation time was at nine o'clock. He glanced at his phone, 8:15. Less than an hour before he was supposed to be off the ship—less than an hour to find one woman among thousands of passengers.

Time was running out.

He jammed his finger against the down button repeatedly, as if that would make the elevator arrive faster. When the doors finally opened, he crammed himself onto the packed car with at least fifteen other people and their luggage, all heading to deck five to disembark. He needed to go two decks lower to the third floor.

Standing inside the crowded elevator, pressed against the back wall by a massive rolling suitcase, he willed the damn machine to move faster. He should have taken the stairs. Why hadn't he taken the stairs?

How was he going to find her when he got there? He didn't know her cabin number. Hadn't thought to ask because he'd been so certain he'd have the morning with her. So sure he'd wake up with her in his arms and they'd exchange numbers over breakfast, make plans, promise to text when they got home.

A little girl wedged next to him glanced down at his bare feet, her eyes widening. "Where are your shoes, mister?"

"I left them in my room. I was in a hurry," he said, barely glancing at her.

"Momma says you should always wear shoes on the ship," she announced with the absolute certainty of a six-year-old quoting gospel. "You can pick up diseases. And foot fungus."

Just what he didn't need, a lecture from a child about hygiene when his entire future happiness might be slipping through his fingers.

With a sigh, he forced himself to look down at the little girl's earnest face. "Your mother is absolutely right. I know better, but I left without thinking. Sometimes adults make dumb choices when they're in a hurry."

The girl shook her head with an expression of profound disappointment, as if she'd expected better from grown-ups.

Her mother gave a barely suppressed snicker from somewhere behind a tower of shopping bags.

Finally, finally, the elevator lurched to a stop on deck five. The doors opened, and three-quarters of the passengers shuffled off with their luggage. Ryan squeezed his way toward the front as the doors closed again. Just two more floors. Two more floors and maybe, maybe, he'd find her.

The elevator seemed to chug down to the third floor with agonizing slowness, as if the machinery itself was conspiring against him. When the doors opened, he burst out into the hallway and then stopped, the reality of his situation hitting him like cold water.

He had no idea how to find her room.

The hall was noticeably vacant compared to the chaos upstairs. It was eerily silent, just the distant hum of machinery and the soft swoosh of doors closing. Only the housekeeping staff and a few stewards moved through the corridors, pushing carts loaded with linens and cleaning supplies.

"Amelia!" he yelled, his voice echoing off the walls. "Amelia!"

A steward in a crisp white uniform appeared from around the corner, concern creasing his face as he approached.

"Can I help you, sir?"

"Yes," Ryan said, hearing the desperation in his own voice and not caring. "Yes, I'm trying to find a woman. Her name is Amelia. She was staying on this floor."

The steward's expression shifted to something between sympathy and wariness. "What's her last name, sir?"

"I don't know." The admission felt like swallowing glass. "That's why I've got to find her before she leaves. Please, can you help me?"

The man sighed and shook his head slowly. "I'm sorry, sir. This floor disembarked at seven-thirty. It's past eight now. I think you're too late."

A sense of regret filled Ryan unlike anything he'd felt in years, not since the night of the accident when he'd realized he'd never see Sandy alive again. How had he overslept the most important morning of his life? How had he let this happen?

"And sir," the steward added, his voice gentler now, "it's against ship regulations to be barefoot in the common areas. I suggest you return to your cabin and prepare for your own departure."

Ryan barely heard him. His mind was racing, trying to figure out another angle. "The ship's records, you must have a passenger manifest. Can you look her up? Just tell me her last name. Or her cabin number. I need to find her."

Why hadn't he gotten her phone number last night? Her last name? Her email address? Anything to let him know who she really was beyond the woman who'd made him feel alive again. He desperately wanted to find her.

"I'll give you fifty dollars if you tell me her last name," he said, pulling out his wallet with shaking hands. "Hell, I'll give you a hundred."

The steward took a step back, his expression hardening. "Sir, that's against ship policy. I'd lose my job if management found out I'd accessed passenger information for personal reasons."

"I would never tell," Ryan said, knowing even as the words left his mouth that he sounded exactly like the kind of stalker women were warned about. "Please. I'm not, this isn't what it looks like. We spent last night together and I just... I need to find her."

The man's face softened slightly, but he shook his head firmly. "I'm sorry. I can't help you."

"What about the main office?" Ryan asked, grasping at straws. "Do you think they would give me her contact information? Or at least contact her for me and give her my name and number? I just want her to know I tried to find her."

The steward glanced down the hallway, then back at Ryan. "I honestly don't know, sir. The guest services desk might be able to help you, but I doubt they'll release passenger information. All you can do is try. They're on deck five."

"Thank you," Ryan said, though the words felt hollow.

The man nodded and walked away, his cart squeaking as he pushed it toward the next cabin.

Dejected, Ryan slumped toward the elevator, his bare feet cold against the industrial carpet. He'd have to go back up to deck five, try the guest services desk, probably get nowhere, then race back to his suite to pack and check out.

But at least he had one piece of information. She'd told him last night, during those quiet conversations between bouts of lovemaking, she was a lawyer. She'd just taken a job in Cheyenne, Wyoming. A fresh start in a new city after a bad breakup that had left her feeling as lonely as he'd been.

How many lawyers named Amelia could be working in Cheyenne? It wasn't New York or Los Angeles. It was a mid-sized city. He could find her. As soon as he got home to Missoula, he'd search the internet. He'd call every law firm in Cheyenne if he had to. He'd show up on her doorstep with flowers and an apology for falling asleep when she'd needed him to stay awake.

An hour later, after throwing his belongings haphazardly into his suitcase and checking out of his suite, Ryan stood in line at the guest services desk on deck five. The queue moved with glacial slowness, people complaining about charges, asking about lost items, requesting receipts for their corporate accounts.

When he finally reached the counter, a professionally pleasant woman in her forties smiled at him. "How can I help you today, sir?"

"I need information about another passenger," he said. "A woman named Amelia. She was staying on deck three. I need her contact information, or I need you to contact her for me and give her my number."

The smile dimmed but didn't disappear. "I'm sorry, sir.

We can't release passenger information due to privacy regulations."

"I understand, but—"

"However," she continued, "if you'd like to leave your contact information, I can make a note in the system. If the passenger in question contacts us looking for you, we can provide them with what you've left."

It was something. Not much, but something.

"Yes," he said. "Please. Her name is Amelia. I don't know her last name. She was on deck three. Tell her Ryan from deck seven is looking for her. Here's my number, my email, everything."

He scribbled his information on the form she provided, his handwriting barely legible in his haste.

The woman took it with a sympathetic smile that told him she'd seen this scenario play out before. "I hope she contacts us, sir. Have a safe journey home."

Thirty minutes later, Ryan disembarked from the ship and caught a shuttle to Miami International Airport. He collapsed into a window seat on the bus, exhaustion finally catching up with him. But beneath the tiredness, something else stirred, determination mixed with hope mixed with bone-deep regret.

Last night had been the best night of his life since the accident. With Amelia, he'd felt an attraction he'd not experienced in years. An easy connection, a natural chemistry, a sense that maybe, just maybe, he could build a life beyond grief and guilt. He'd wanted so desperately to continue what they'd started, to see if the magic of last night could survive in daylight.

But he'd lost the opportunity through his own stupidity.

He wanted to kick himself for falling asleep. And yet, paradoxically, he'd slept better last night than he had in three years. Deep, dreamless sleep with Amelia warm in his arms. The sleep of someone who'd finally let go of the past enough to embrace the present.

His only real chance of finding Amelia was to check the law offices in Cheyenne. Maybe there he would find her. Hell, Cheyenne wasn't that far from Missoula. just under six hours if he drove straight through. He'd even take vacation days and drive down there if that's what it took to locate her.

Whatever was necessary, he had to find her.

Because somehow, in the space of one night, Amelia had reminded him what it felt like to be alive. And he wasn't ready to let that feeling go.

CHAPTER 4

$\mathcal{F}$our Days before Christmas Eve

The satellite radio cut in and out as Amelia drove, the signal fragmenting mid-chorus. She'd been singing along to "Silent Night" when the static took over, a fitting metaphor for her life lately. Through the windshield, snowflakes spiraled in her headlights like tiny dancers performing just for her, their choreography growing more frantic with each passing mile.

She adjusted her grip on the steering wheel, her hands already aching from the tension. Just a few more hours. That's what she'd been telling herself for the past two hundred miles, but the storm had other plans.

Her family would be overjoyed to see her. She could already picture her mother's face lighting up, her father pulling her into one of his bear hugs that somehow always made everything feel manageable. They'd fuss over her, ask why she hadn't called more, they'd notice she looked different somehow, though, until she took her coat off, they wouldn't immediately guess why.

Because the golden girl had a secret.

And not just any secret. The kind that would make her mother cry, happy tears, eventually, but shocked ones first. The kind that would make her father go silent in that dangerous way he had before erupting into a speech about responsibility and consequences, even though she was thirty-two years old and a successful attorney who'd just made junior partner.

Former junior partner, technically. But they didn't need to know that part yet either.

A gust of wind slammed into her SUV, and she white-knuckled the wheel, her heart hammering. The snowflakes had stopped dancing. Now they were attacking, coming at her windshield in thick, furious sheets that her wipers could barely keep up with.

"Come on," she muttered, squinting at the road ahead. At this rate, she wouldn't reach Whitefish until well past midnight.

The visibility dropped to almost nothing. One moment she could see the faint outline of the road; the next, everything was white. Pure, blinding white.

She needed to get home tonight. Needed her mother's arms around her, needed to hear her father's stern voice asking if she'd lost her mind, and for once, she'd agree with him. Yes, Dad. Yes, I've absolutely lost my mind. But it's the best kind of crazy, the kind that fills your heart so full you think it might burst.

She hadn't felt this way since Tommy Mercer kissed her behind the bleachers sophomore year, when the whole world seemed to shimmer with possibility.

Her parents would understand. Eventually. They might be traditional, might wish she'd done things in a different order, but they'd love her through it. That's what the Millers did, they loved you through your mistakes, your detours, your beautiful disasters.

God knew they'd had plenty of practice with Olivia. Her younger sister could find trouble in an empty room.

And Emma. Sweet, scattered Emma. Her twin was probably home already, holed up in their childhood bedroom with a stack of library books and that dreamy expression she got when she was reading a medical textbook. They'd been inseparable once, finishing each other's sentences, feeling each other's pain. But somewhere in their twenties they'd drifted, pulled apart by different career paths and different lives.

Amelia missed her. Missed both her sisters, actually, even Olivia's chaos.

Once she got home, once they saw her, really saw her, she'd be surrounded by their love again. They'd pepper her with questions, bring her tea and blankets, rub her swollen feet, and tell her everything would be fine.

And it would be. She wasn't afraid.

Not yet, anyway.

The highway sign emerged from the white like an orange ghost, its message blinking urgently: **ROAD CLOSED AHEAD. SEEK SHELTER IMMEDIATELY.**

"No." The word came out as a whimper. "No, no, no."

But the next sign confirmed it, and the one after that. By the time she reached the outskirts of Missoula, traffic cones forced her off the interstate entirely.

A blizzard. A genuine, highway-closing, Christmas-ruining blizzard.

She blinked back tears, hormone-fueled, she told herself, though that wasn't entirely true, and started scanning for hotels. Not just any hotel. She needed somewhere clean, somewhere safe. Somewhere with room service because she was starving again, always starving these days. Maybe they'd even have a spa. A massage sounded like heaven. Her back had been screaming for the last hundred miles.

The first hotel, a gleaming luxury property she'd stayed at once for a legal conference, loomed ahead. She pulled under the covered entrance, hope fluttering in her chest.

A valet in a crisp uniform appeared at her window before she could even shift into park. "I'm so sorry, ma'am. We're completely full."

"Right. Thank you."

She pulled away, hands trembling now. What if every-where was full? What if she ended up sleeping in her car, in a blizzard, with a baby doing somersaults against her ribcage?

Four hotels later, she was trying not to panic. The fifth was a mid-range chain that looked clean enough. She parked under the awning and heaved herself out of the driver's seat, wincing as her legs protested. Her feet had swollen so much that her boots felt two sizes too small. The extra forty pounds she was carrying made everything harder, getting in and out of the car, bending down, breathing.

She waddled toward the entrance. God, she actually waddled now, grateful when the automatic doors swooshed open. Her belly passed through first, arriving at destinations a full second before the rest of her.

The lobby was warm and bright and smelled like cinnamon. Christmas music played softly. Under other circumstances, it would have felt cozy.

The desk clerk looked up with an apologetic smile that Amelia recognized immediately. She knew that smile.

"Please tell me you have a room," Amelia said anyway, even though she already knew.

"I'm so sorry, ma'am. We're sold out."

"Damn it."

The word came out sharper than intended, and then the pain hit.

It started low, a tightening sensation that spread across her entire belly like someone was wrapping her midsection in a vice grip and slowly, methodically, cranking it tighter.

She gasped, one hand flying to her stomach, the other grabbing the edge of the desk.

"Ma'am? Are you okay?"

She couldn't answer. All her focus went to breathing, slow inhale through the nose, slow exhale through the mouth, just like they'd taught her in the birthing class she'd taken alone while pretending to text someone in the parking lot afterward so she wouldn't look quite so pathetic.

This couldn't be labor. It was too early. Two weeks too early. She wasn't home yet. She didn't have her mother. She didn't have anyone.

"I'm calling 911," the clerk said, her voice rising with alarm.

A security guard materialized at her elbow, his hand gentle on her arm. "Ma'am, you need to sit down. You've gone white as a ghost."

She wanted to explain that she couldn't sit, couldn't move, couldn't do anything except breathe and count. Twenty-five, twenty-six, twenty-seven...

Thirty seconds. The contraction lasted thirty seconds before it began to ease, the vice grip loosening incrementally until she could stand up straight again.

Was this it? Was she actually in labor, or was this another false alarm like the one she'd had last week that had sent her to the ER at two in the morning only to be sent home embarrassed?

They guided her to a long leather sofa, and she sank into it gratefully, then immediately realized she might not be able to get back up without assistance. The cushions seemed to swallow her whole.

The desk clerk hurried over, her name tag reading "Patricia." She looked about fifty, with kind eyes and the competent air of someone who'd seen everything.

"Is this your first?" Patricia asked.

"Yes." Amelia's voice came out thready, weak. "I think I'm okay. I just need to find a hotel and—"

"Honey, there are no hotel rooms in Missoula. Not a single one." Patricia's expression was sympathetic but firm. "This storm came in faster than they predicted. Highway patrol closed all the roads over two hours ago. Every stranded traveler in a hundred-mile radius ended up here. We were full an hour ago."

Two hours. She'd missed the window by two hours.

If she'd left Cheyenne yesterday like she'd planned, she'd be home now. But she'd had to tie up loose ends at the firm, had to finish that last brief, had to pretend everything was fine even though she was about to blow up her entire life.

Thirteen hours. The drive should have taken thirteen hours, but she'd needed to stop constantly, bathroom breaks every hour, a lunch break that turned into a nap, another bathroom break, another snack. Her bladder had been the size of a peanut for months.

Just two more hours separated her from home. Two more hours on increasingly treacherous roads.

What was she thinking? She had a baby to consider now.

But was she willing to risk her baby?

The thought hit her like a physical blow, and suddenly her eyes were burning with tears. Bad things didn't happen to her. She was Amelia Miller, straight A's, full scholarship, law review, junior partner. Blessed. Charmed. Lucky.

Except this year had been a series of catastrophes

masquerading as life lessons. The miscarriage of justice in the Morrison case still kept her up at night. The betrayal by her mentor, who'd stolen her work and presented it as his own.

The firing three weeks ago, dressed up in corporate language about "work quality not meeting firm standards," as if she hadn't won every major case she'd touched. As if they thought she was stupid enough not to know the real reason. She'd seen the looks, heard the whispered conversations that stopped when she entered the conference room. The golden girl had committed the cardinal sin: she'd gotten pregnant without permission, without a husband, without fitting into their neat little boxes of what a successful woman attorney should be.

And through it all, this baby. This unplanned, unexpected, utterly wanted baby.

The pregnancy had been an accident, obviously. But somewhere around week twelve, when she'd heard the heartbeat for the first time, that rapid-fire whooshing sound like a tiny helicopter, it had stopped being an accident and started being her purpose.

This baby was hers. The father had been wonderful, though she had no way to contact him and wasn't even sure she wanted to. How could she blame him when he didn't know? One night, one celebration, one connection so intense it had left her shaking. Just a memory of emerald eyes and a smile that made her forget to be careful.

She hoped the baby had his eyes.

"Ma'am? Are you all right?"

Patricia's voice pulled her back to the present. "Yes. I think so."

But then another contraction seized her, and she gasped, all the air leaving her lungs in a rush.

"Breathe through it," Patricia coached, crouching beside her. "Nice and slow. That's it."

When the pain crested and began to subside, Patricia helped her to her feet. "Come on. Walk with me. Movement helps."

They walked the length of the lobby and back, Patricia's hand firm on her elbow. Through the windows, the storm raged, snow piling up in drifts against the glass.

"It's too early," Amelia said, hearing the panic in her own voice. "I'm not due for two more weeks."

Patricia's eyes widened. "What are you doing out on the road? Where's your husband?"

The question hit harder than the contractions. Amelia felt fresh tears spilling down her cheeks, hot against her cold skin.

There was no husband. No boyfriend. No partner of any kind. Just her and this baby and a life she was trying to figure out one day at a time.

The lawyers at her firm had stopped looking at her altogether once her belly became obvious. The men she'd once considered friends had suddenly become distant, professional. It was like pregnancy had rendered her invisible, or worse, inconvenient. Right up until they'd called her into that conference room and told her she was no longer needed.

"The father doesn't know," she finally managed to say between breaths. "But it's okay. This baby is mine."

Patricia squeezed her arm. "Men can be heartless."

Amelia didn't want to think of him that way. Didn't want to poison his memory with resentment he hadn't earned. "It was an accident," she said. "But I decided to keep her. She's my beautiful little accident."

Patricia smiled at that. "Have you chosen a name?"

"Not yet. I want to name her after my grandmother, but I'm waiting until I get home. Until I can talk to my mother and father."

The tears came faster now, harder to control. She'd been so close. So close to being home, to telling her parents face-to-face, to seeing their faces when they realized they were about to become grandparents.

The automatic doors whooshed open, letting in a blast of arctic air and three figures in the most ridiculous costumes Amelia had ever seen.

Santa Claus, or someone in a surprisingly authentic Santa suit, strode in carrying a walkie-talkie, flanked by two "elves" in green and red striped tights who were carrying a stretcher between them.

The handful of people scattered around the lobby burst into applause and laughter.

Santa approached the desk. "Someone call for an ambulance?"

"Yes," Patricia said, gesturing toward Amelia. "I think she's in labor."

He turned around, and the world tilted.

Those eyes. Those impossible emerald eyes she'd been dreaming about for nine months.

"Ryan?"

His face went through several expressions in rapid succession, confusion, recognition, shock, and something that might have been joy before it was swallowed by panic.

"Amelia? What the hell are you doing here?"

"I'm pregnant," she said, as if he couldn't see that for himself. And burst out crying.

CHAPTER 5

*D*ear God, the woman Ryan had spent nine months searching for was standing in front of him. Right here, in a hotel lobby in Missoula, on the worst night of the year.

And she was pregnant.

Very, very pregnant.

His brain stuttered, trying to process what his eyes were seeing. Unless she'd immediately jumped into bed with someone else after their night together, and everything in him rejected that possibility, the baby she was carrying was his.

Joy and terror hit him simultaneously, a one-two punch that left him struggling to breathe inside the ridiculous Santa suit. The fake beard itched. The padding around his middle felt suffocating. And everyone in the lobby was staring at them like they were the evening's entertainment.

This was not the place to have this conversation. This

was not the place to ask the thousand questions rico-cheting through his mind. And yet it took every ounce of his professional training to keep from grabbing her shoulders and demanding, *Is that child mine?*

Focus. He had to focus.

"Are you certain these aren't Braxton Hicks?" he asked, forcing his voice into the calm, measured tone he used with all his patients. "Has your water broken? How far along are you?"

"I'm thirty-eight weeks." Her voice trembled. "And no, my water hasn't broken."

Thirty-eight weeks.

The math was simple, brutal, undeniable. That child, that sweet child nestled in her rounded belly. was his.

They'd used condoms. He remembered that clearly, remembered being careful even through the haze of want and whiskey and the way she'd looked at him like he was the only man in the world. But condoms weren't foolproof. He knew that. He'd responded to enough calls over the years, had seen enough surprised parents, to know that protection sometimes failed.

And apparently, theirs had.

"Do you mind if I listen to your stomach?" He was already reaching for his stethoscope, needing to confirm what his heart already knew.

"Go ahead."

Her eyes stayed locked on his face as he pressed the stethoscope to her belly. The lobby noise faded to white static. All he could hear was the rapid flutter of a heartbeat, strong, steady, perfect.

His child. His baby.

His own heart hammered so loudly he was amazed he could hear anything else.

He pulled the stethoscope away, suddenly aware that his hands were shaking. "Are you staying here?"

"No." She shook her head, looking miserable and exhausted and more beautiful than he remembered. "I stopped to rent a room when the contraction started."

"Has it stopped now?"

"Yes."

"She had a second bout of pain a little bit ago," the clerk, Patricia, according to her name tag, interjected. She was hovering nearby, clearly invested in the drama unfolding in her lobby.

Ryan wrapped the blood pressure cuff around Amelia's arm, needing something to do with his hands, needing to stay professional even though his entire world had just tilted sideways. "Where's your husband?"

He knew the answer. Had known it the moment he'd recognized her. But he needed to hear it.

"No husband."

The silence stretched between them as he pumped the cuff, watched the numbers climb, tried to ignore the way her pulse jumped beneath his fingers.

One forty over ninety.

His stomach dropped.

That was high. Too high for a pregnant woman this far along. Fear lanced through him, cold and sharp. Preeclampsia was no joke. Women died from it. Babies died from it.

He pulled the stethoscope from his ears and took her hand, unable to stop himself. Her fingers were cold, slightly swollen.

"Your blood pressure is one forty over ninety. That's high for a pregnant woman." He kept his voice gentle, calm, even though his mind was racing through worst-case scenarios. "You're alone?"

"Yes." The word came out small, scared.

He could see the terror in her eyes, the same terror that was clawing at his own chest. He wanted to pull her into his arms, wanted to promise her that everything would be fine, that he would take care of her and their baby. But first, he needed to get her to the hospital. Needed a doctor to examine her, to make sure she wasn't in immediate danger.

He was not about to lose Amelia or this child. Not when he'd just found them.

"We're out of rooms, Santa," Patricia said, drawing his attention. "She has no place to stay."

Ryan felt his jaw tighten. "She's nine months pregnant with high blood pressure, alone, and driving in a storm." He couldn't keep the incredulity out of his voice. "What were you thinking?"

Amelia flinched, and immediately he regretted his tone. This wasn't the time for recriminations. Her blood pressure was already too high, getting her upset would only make it worse.

"Where are you headed?" he asked, gentler this time.

"Whitefish, Montana." Fresh tears spilled down her cheeks. "I'm so close. I just want to be with my mother and father and family for Christmas."

Whitefish. Two hours north in good weather, but in this storm? Impossible. The roads were closed. Even if they weren't, he wouldn't let her get back in that car if his life depended on it.

He stood and motioned to Jake and Marcus, his partner and trainee, who'd been hanging back with the stretcher. "Because your blood pressure is high, I think we should take you to the hospital and get you examined."

"The baby is all right?" The panic in her voice nearly undid him.

He reached for her hand again, squeezed it gently. The warmth of her skin against his felt like coming home. "We're going to make certain that you and the baby are just fine. Everything seems normal, but I want a doctor to check you out. We don't want you coming down with preeclampsia. It's not quite time for that little one to arrive, so we want to keep him or her cooking a little longer."

He paused, making sure she was listening, making sure she understood. "And since you're alone, I'm not willing to let you get back in your car."

She bit her lip, a gesture he remembered from that night, and sighed. "The doctor warned me about preeclampsia, about the symptoms to watch for. I've been in the car for over eleven hours. Maybe that's why my blood pressure is high."

Over eleven hours. Driving alone, nine months pregnant, stopping God knew how many times, probably not eating properly or staying hydrated. The urge to lecture her was overwhelming, but he swallowed it down. Getting angry wouldn't help anyone.

He glanced down at her feet, noting the way they strained against her boots. "Your feet are puffy and swollen. Not a good sign. Are you agreeable to going to the hospital?"

"Will you be there?"

The way she asked, tentative, hopeful, made something in his chest crack open.

"I wouldn't be anywhere else." He meant it with every fiber of his being. "Not even the children's Christmas party will keep me from being with you."

"You can't miss that." She looked genuinely distressed. "Those kids—"

"We'll see," he interrupted, unwilling to make promises about Santa when his own child might be in danger. "First, let's get you to the ER."

She glanced around the lobby, at the small crowd that had gathered to watch the spectacle, then nodded. "What about my car? It's still parked in the drive."

"I'll get it moved for you," Patricia said, already reaching for the keys Amelia was fumbling out of her purse.

This was real. This was actually happening.

Ryan moved closer, keeping his voice soft so only she

could hear. "What's your last name, Amelia? I've wondered for months. I've looked everywhere for you."

"Miller." She looked up at him as he helped her ease back onto the stretcher, and something in her expression made his throat tight. "Amelia Miller."

"I'm Ryan Allen," he said, managing a smile despite everything. "Your friendly Santa paramedic."

She smiled back, a real smile this time, small but genuine. "Why are you dressed that way?"

"We were on our way to a children's Christmas party when dispatch told us they were backed up with all the accidents on the roads. We weren't far from the hotel, so they sent us." He secured the strap across her chest, trying not to think about how many times he'd imagined finding her again, and how none of those scenarios had looked anything like this. "Thank God they did."

Thank God. Because what if they hadn't taken this call? What if another unit had responded? What if he'd never found her, never learned about his child?

The alternative was too terrible to consider.

"I'm so sorry," Amelia said as they began rolling the gurney toward the door. "I don't want the children to miss out."

"It comes with the territory." He shrugged, though his hands were shaking as he helped guide the stretcher through the lobby. "We were just going to show up and hand out presents. They'll understand."

The cold air hit them like a slap when they emerged from the hotel. Snow was still falling in thick curtains, and Ryan could barely see the ambulance parked at the curb.

Part of him was angry that she hadn't contacted him. But that anger dissolved almost as quickly as it formed. He'd been searching for her for nine months, unable to find any trace. Maybe it had been the same for her. Had he even told her where he lived that night? They'd talked about so many things between kisses, between touches, but had he mentioned Missoula? He couldn't remember.

Jake and Marcus helped load the stretcher into the ambulance, their movements practiced and efficient. Patricia appeared beside them, pressing Amelia's purse into Ryan's hands.

"Good luck," she called over the wind. "Let me know if you have the baby!"

Ryan climbed in beside Amelia, ignoring Jake's raised eyebrow. Normally he rode up front or let his team handle transport while he moved on to the next call. But there was no way, absolutely no way, he was letting anyone else handle this one.

They secured the stretcher, and Ryan pounded twice on the wall separating them from the cab. "Let's get this sled rolling to Missoula General!"

The ambulance lurched into motion, and Ryan sank onto the bench seat beside her. For a moment, he just looked at her. really looked at her. The curve of her belly beneath the stretcher strap. The exhaustion etched in her face. The fear in her eyes that probably mirrored his own.

He took her hand again, unable to stop himself.

"I have to ask." His voice came out rougher than he intended. "Is this child mine?"

A tear rolled down her cheek, catching the harsh ambulance lighting. "Yes. I tried to find you, but I had no luck."

Relief and regret hit him in equal measure. "I tried to find you, too." The memory of that morning still stung. "When I woke up and you were gone, I ran up and down the third floor barefoot, barely dressed, screaming your name until the steward told me that everyone on that floor had already disembarked."

Now she was crying harder, her shoulders shaking. "I'm sorry, Ryan. We used protection. And then I couldn't find you either."

"We did use protection," he agreed, squeezing her hand. "But it's kind of odd that you're the last stop my ambulance made today. Like the universe meant for us to find each other."

"You're not mad?"

"Hell no." The words came out fierce, emphatic. "I'm thrilled. I'm excited." His voice softened. "I just wish I'd been with you all nine months."

She wiped her eyes with her free hand, leaving mascara smudges on her cheek that he wanted to brush away.

"But what in the hell were you doing out driving?" The question came out harsher than he intended. "At nine months pregnant, in a blizzard?"

"I wanted to go home for Christmas." Her voice broke. "No one in my family knows I'm pregnant. I've been so alone."

The words hit him like a physical blow. He thought of Sandy's pregnancy with Emma, how needy she'd been, how he'd had to be there for every doctor's appointment, every craving, every moment of panic. And Amelia had done it all alone. No partner. No support.

Because of him. Because he hadn't found her in time.

"Not anymore," he said firmly. "I'm going to be by your side."

"Are you certain?" She searched his face, looking for doubt. "We only had one night together."

"Only because you didn't leave your last name and phone number," he pointed out.

"I wasn't certain what to do. I didn't know if you wanted to continue what we started."

"How could you not have realized that you were the best thing that happened to me in two years?" The confession came out raw, honest.

She gave a small laugh that ended in a hiccup. "Maybe because we didn't talk much. All we did was express our needs with our bodies."

That was true. Once they'd reached his suite, conversation had become impossible. They'd communicated in touches, in gasps, in the way their bodies fit together like they'd been designed for each other. When they'd finally collapsed, exhausted and sated, he'd fallen into the deepest sleep he'd had since before Sandy died.

"We'll talk more," he promised. "But just realize that this child is a part of me. A part of me that I want to be involved with." He paused, then added what he was really thinking. "And you're not going anywhere."

She stiffened immediately, and he knew he'd pushed too hard, too fast.

"I'm going home for Christmas."

Her voice was flat, final. Not a request, a statement. He recognized that tone. Sandy had used it whenever she'd made up her mind about something. Arguing would only make things worse, and would only drive her blood pressure higher.

"We'll wait and see what the doctor has to say," he said carefully. "That baby is your top priority. Everything else can wait."

"I'm going home for Christmas," she repeated, and he could hear the stubbornness beneath the exhaustion.

Great. His child's mother had a spine of steel.

Somehow, that didn't surprise him at all.

The ambulance hit a pothole and Amelia winced, her hand tightening on his. Through the small window, he could see nothing but swirling white. The storm showed no signs of letting up.

He looked down at their joined hands, at the woman who'd haunted his dreams for nine months, at the belly that held his child.

Whatever happened next, whatever the doctor said, whatever Amelia decided about Christmas or Whitefish or anything else, he wasn't letting her go again.

He'd spent nine months searching for her.

Now that he'd found her, he was going to fight like hell to keep her.

Dear God, the woman he'd spent the last nine months searching for was here. Right here in Missoula and she was pregnant. And unless she'd gone out and gotten pregnant immediately after the cruise, that baby she was carrying was his.

Happiness and terror gripped him and he realized that everyone in the hotel lobby was staring at them. This was not the place for them to talk, and yet, it was all he could do to keep from screaming *is that child mine?*

"Are you certain these aren't Braxton Hicks?" he asked her, doing his best to remain professional. "Has your water broken? How far along are you?"

"I'm thirty-eight weeks," she said. "And no, my water has not broken."

Thirty-eight weeks. That sweet child nestled in her belly was his. But they'd used condoms that night. No, condoms were not foolproof and it appeared that they were going to experience what a broken condom could create.

Focus. He had to focus on his job.

"Do you mind if I listen to your stomach?"

"Go ahead," she said.

She watched as he put the stethoscope to her belly and listened to the baby. Their baby. His child. His heart pounded so loudly in his chest that it was a wonder he could hear the fetus.

Pulling the stethoscope from around his ears, he glanced at her. "Are you staying here?"

"No," she said. "I stopped to rent a room when the contraction started."

"Has it stopped now?"

"Yes," she said.

"She had a second bout of pain a little bit ago," the clerk told him.

"Where's your husband?" he asked, fairly certain there wasn't one as he placed a blood pressure cuff on her arm.

That was his child.

"No husband."

For a moment, they were quiet as he took her blood pressure and pulse. Fear seized him as he realized the implications and how she could even now be in danger. Staring at her, he pulled the stethoscope from his ears and took her hand.

"Your blood pressure is one forty over ninety. That's high for a pregnant woman. You're alone?"

"Yes," she said, gazing at him. He saw the terror in her eyes. Somehow he had to make her realize that he would take care of her and their baby. When they were alone, they would talk, but now he needed to get her to the hospital and get her checked out.

He was not about to lose Amelia or this child.

"We're out of rooms, Santa. She has no place to stay," the clerk said. "She's nine months pregnant with high blood pressure, alone, and driving in a storm. What a bad idea."

What the hell was she doing out on the road alone at nine months pregnant? She should be at home with her feet propped up, someone taking care of her. And that someone was damn well going to be him. But first, he had to reassure her. It wouldn't be good for her blood pressure to rise any higher.

"Where are you headed?"

"Whitefish, Montana. I'm so close," she said. "I just want to be with my mother and father and family for Christmas."

Standing, he motioned for the guys who had unloaded the stretcher. "Because your blood pressure is high, I think we should take you to the hospital and get you examined."

She started to cry. "The baby is all right?"

He reached out and took her hand in his. Warmth filled him. They were having a baby. This woman that he'd searched so hard for was here in front of him, and he would do everything he could to take care of her.

"We're going to make certain that you and baby are just fine. Everything appears normal, but I want a doctor to look at you. We don't want you coming down with preeclampsia. It's not quite time for that little one to arrive, so we want to keep him or her in the oven a little longer. And since you're alone, I'm not willing to let you get back in your car."

Biting her lip, she sighed. "The doctor warned me about the disease and the symptoms. I've been in the car for over eleven hours. Maybe that's why my blood pressure is high."

For a moment, he wanted to throttle her but knew that

would do no good. It would be best if he stayed calm and got her to the hospital. After that, he was going to convince her to stay with him.

"Your feet are puffy and swollen. Not a good sign," he told her. "Are you agreeable to going to the hospital?"

"Will you be there?"

The way she asked gave him hope.

"I wouldn't be anywhere else. Not even the children's Christmas party will keep me from being with you."

"You can't miss that," she said.

How could he play Santa when his own child might be in danger?

"We'll see," he said. "First, let's get you to the ER."

Glancing around, she nodded. "What about my car? It's still parked in the drive of the hotel."

"I'll get it moved for you," the clerk said as she handed Amelia her purse. She found her keys and handed them to the clerk

"What's your last name, Amelia? I've wondered for months," he said soft and low. "I've looked everywhere for you."

"Miller," she said as he took her hand and helped her lie back on the stretcher.

"I'm Ryan Allen," he said. "Your friendly Santa paramedic."

She smiled at him. "Why are you dressed that way?"

"We were on our way to a children's Christmas party when dispatch told us they were backed up with all the accidents on the roads and we weren't far from the hotel."

Thank God they had answered this call. What if he'd never found her? What if he'd never learned about his sweet baby?

"I'm so sorry," she said. "I don't want the children to miss out."

They rolled the gurney through the lobby and finally out the door.

He shrugged. "It comes with the territory. We were going to just show up and hand out presents."

His hands shook as they loaded her into the ambulance. Part of him was angry that she hadn't contacted him. But he'd been searching for her and unable to locate her. Maybe it was the same for her. That night, had he told her where he lived?

Once they had her secured in the ambulance, the clerk handed him her purse and he crawled in beside her. There was no way he was going to let one of his guys handle this one.

"Good luck. Let me know if you have the baby," she said.

They shut the ambulance doors, locked down the stretcher, and then Ryan hit the back of the wagon. "Let's get this sled rolling to Missoula General."

Once they were on the road, he took her hand. "I have to ask, is this child mine?"

A tear rolled down her cheek. "Yes. I tried to find you, but I had no luck."

Just as he thought.

"I tried to find you as well," he said. "That morning

when I awoke, I ran up and down the third floor barefoot, barely dressed, screaming your name until the steward told me that everyone on that floor had already left."

Now she was crying harder. "I'm sorry, Ryan. We used protection. And then I couldn't find you."

"We did use protection," he said. "It's kind of odd that you are the last stop my ambulance made today. It's like the universe meant for us to find each other."

"You're not mad?"

"Hell no," he said. "I'm thrilled. I'm excited. I just wish I'd been with you all nine months."

She wiped her eyes with her free hand.

"But what in the hell were you doing out driving?"

"I wanted to go home for Christmas," she said. "No one in my family knows I'm pregnant. I've been so alone."

His heart wrenched at her words as he remembered Sandy's pregnancy and how needy and hormonal she'd been. And yet, Amelia had done it all alone.

"Not anymore," he said. "I'm going to be by your side."

"Are you certain?" she said. "We only had the one night."

"Only because you didn't leave your last name and phone number," he said.

"I wasn't certain what to do. I didn't know if you wanted to continue," she said.

"Oh my God. How could you not have realized that you were the best thing that has happened to me in two years?"

She gave a little giggle. "Maybe because we didn't talk much. All we did was express our needs with our bodies."

That was true. Once they reached his suite, it had been

on like Donkey Kong. They had barely come up for air, and then exhausted, he'd fallen into the best sleep he'd experienced in years.

"We'll talk more, but just realize that this child is a part of me. A part of me that I want to be involved with. And you're not going anywhere."

She tensed and he knew that had not been the right thing to say. But if he had his way, she would stay right here in Missoula until this baby was born and maybe even forever if he could convince her to stay.

"I'm going home for Christmas," she said.

It would be best not to argue with her. It would only cause her blood pressure to rise.

"We'll wait and see what the doctor has to say," he said. "That baby is your top priority. Everything else can wait."

"I'm going home for Christmas," she repeated and he realized she had a stubborn streak.

CHAPTER 6

Amelia hadn't driven thirteen hours through increasingly terrible weather just to give up two hours from home. She was going to make it to Whitefish for Christmas. She had to.

She wanted her mother at the birth. Needed her mother, the woman who'd guided her through every milestone, every crisis, every triumph. She wanted her sisters there, even chaotic Olivia with her unsolicited advice and Emma with her quiet, steady presence. She wanted to be surrounded by the people who'd loved her since before she could walk.

And now, she also wanted Ryan.

He was her baby's father. She'd tried so hard to find him, spent hours scrolling through social media, contacted the cruise line three times, even hired a private investigator who'd come up empty. Without a last name, it had been impossible.

The irony wasn't lost on her. She'd searched for him desperately, and he'd been right here in Missoula all along. Just two hours from home. If she'd taken that job offer from Patterson & Associates last year, the one she'd turned down because Cheyenne's firm was more prestigious, more impressive on a resume, she might have run into him at a coffee shop months ago. They could have figured this out together from the beginning.

But no. She'd chosen the conservative firm in Cheyenne, the one with the mahogany offices and the leather-bound law books and the old white men who'd made it very clear they didn't approve of her situation. Unmarried. Pregnant. A stain on their reputation.

They'd fired her with such careful language. "Your work is not the quality our firm is looking for." As if she hadn't won the Morrison case. As if she hadn't billed more hours than any other junior partner. As if her pregnancy hadn't been showing for three weeks before they'd called her into that conference room.

It was a complete lie, but honestly? She didn't care anymore.

The Morrison settlement had been substantial, and her cut had been enough to live on for several months. She'd spent the last two months at home in sweats, sending out resumes, researching family law firms, building a plan for after the baby came. She'd be fine. Better than fine, she'd be free of their judgment.

Pregnant and fired in nine months. Her previously charmed life had certainly lost some of its shine. Olivia and

Emma would probably find it hilarious once they got over the shock. The golden girl, finally tarnished.

But losing her job wasn't important. Not compared to this baby. As long as her little accident was born healthy, nothing else mattered.

And Ryan was holding her hand like he never wanted to let go, looking at her like she was something precious, and it felt good. It felt right in a way nothing had felt right in months.

When they arrived at the hospital, he turned to her, his expression serious beneath the ridiculous fake beard. "You have to tell them this is my child, or they won't allow me in the room."

She nodded, suddenly overwhelmed by the reality of it. Every doctor's appointment, she'd been alone. Every ultrasound, every blood draw, every moment of fear, alone. Even the birthing classes, where she'd pretended to text someone in the parking lot afterward so she wouldn't look quite so pathetic walking to her car by herself.

It would be different now. She could see it in his eyes, he wanted to be part of this. Part of their baby's life.

The two paramedics who'd ridden up front, Stan and Adam, she'd heard Ryan call them, opened the ambulance doors. Cold air rushed in, making her shiver.

"Fellas, I'm officially off duty," Ryan announced. "I'll do my best to make it to the children's party, but right now, Amelia is my priority."

Stan looked between them, a slow grin spreading across his face. "This is Amelia? *The* Amelia?"

"Yes." Ryan's answering grin was incandescent. "I finally found her."

"Thank God," Stan said, shaking his head. "You were driving us all crazy talking about her nonstop."

Adam's eyes widened as he took in her belly. "This is the woman from the cruise? And she's pregnant..."

"With my child," Ryan said as they pulled the stretcher out of the ambulance.

Heat flooded Amelia's cheeks. Nine months of secrecy, and now her situation was being announced to strangers in a hospital parking lot.

"Congratulations, Amelia and Ryan," Stan said warmly as they lowered the stretcher and locked it into position.

"Who knew we'd find each other like this?" she managed, trying to smile through her embarrassment.

Ryan walked beside her as they wheeled her toward the emergency entrance, clearing the path. People smiled at him, at Santa Claus trudging through the snow. Some even called out greetings. If the situation weren't so surreal, it might have been funny.

A nurse met them at the door, her expression shifting from professional to surprised as Ryan rattled off vitals, blood pressure, pulse, and contraction timing. They wheeled her into an exam room and transferred her to a bed with practiced efficiency.

Stan and Adam left, rolling the empty stretcher between them. The nurse, her name tag read "Jennifer"— looked from Ryan to Amelia and back again.

"Santa, why are you still here?"

"He's the father," Amelia said quickly.

Jennifer's mouth fell open. "Oh."

"This is Amelia," Ryan said, still holding Amelia's hand. "The girl I've been searching for since I went on that cruise nine months ago."

Jennifer shook her head, a smile breaking through her shock. "I'm glad you finally found her, but this is quite the surprise."

"For both of us," Ryan agreed. "A good surprise."

"A very good surprise," Amelia added, squeezing his hand.

Jennifer wrapped the blood pressure cuff around Amelia's arm again. "How many weeks?"

"Thirty-eight."

The cuff tightened, released. Jennifer's frown told Amelia everything she needed to know before the nurse even spoke. "Still high. The doctor should be in soon. At thirty-eight weeks, you could deliver with a high probability of the baby being fine, but we'd rather wait a bit longer if possible." She made notes on her tablet. "Let's see what the doctor thinks. I'm going to help you get into a gown. Do you want Ryan to stay or leave?"

Amelia glanced at Ryan, at the hope and concern warring in his expression. "He can stay."

He'd already been up close and personal with every inch of her body. A hospital gown wasn't going to change that.

After Jennifer helped her change and left them alone,

Ryan moved closer to the bed, reclaiming her hand. His grip was firm, warm, anchoring.

"Never expected to see you again this way," he said softly.

"No. Believe me, it was a shock for me too." She studied his face, looking for doubt, for regret, for any sign that his supportive words in the ambulance had just been paramedic professionalism. "I was afraid for a moment. That you'd be angry."

"No." His voice was fierce. "There's no reason to be afraid. I'd been searching for you for months. I'm thrilled you're having our child. I just wish I'd been there from the beginning."

"Me too," she whispered.

Ten minutes felt like an eternity, but finally the doctor walked in, a man in his fifties with kind eyes and a knowing smile. He glanced at Ryan's Santa suit and chuckled.

"Hello, Santa Claus. I hear you two are expecting. Looks like very soon."

"Yes, sir," Ryan said.

Amelia shifted uncomfortably, suddenly aware that everyone in this hospital knew Ryan. Worked with him daily. They hadn't had a chance to talk privately, to figure out what this meant, to establish whether he was just putting on a brave front or if he truly wanted to be part of this.

The awkwardness of it all probably wasn't helping her blood pressure.

She took a deep breath, forcing herself to focus. Right now, the baby was all that mattered. Two more weeks. Just two more weeks, and then this child would be welcomed into the world, and everything else could be sorted out.

"Do you mind if I examine you?" the doctor asked.

"No, go ahead."

The exam was brief, professional. When he finished, he smiled reassuringly. "You're barely dilated. That baby's not quite ready to make an appearance. I think you were having Braxton Hicks contractions because you pushed yourself too hard today, too many hours in the car, not enough movement. That's why your blood pressure is elevated, too." He helped her sit up. "How far are you from home?"

Ryan's hand found hers again, steadying her.

"Two hours away. Whitefish." She looked between the doctor and Ryan, willing them to understand. "I really want to spend Christmas with my family. They don't know about the baby yet, about any of this. I want to have her there, with my mother beside me." Her gaze found Ryan's. "And you too. I just... I'd planned on being with my family."

The doctor nodded slowly. "Well, until this storm passes, you're not going anywhere. The highways are closed. And even when they open, I don't want you driving to Whitefish alone."

Amelia's heart sank.

"However," he continued, "if the roads clear and Ryan agrees to drive you, and you make frequent stops, I'll approve it. But your blood pressure has to come down first, and that swelling in your feet needs to improve."

Hope flickered back to life in her chest.

"So here's the plan." The doctor ticked items off on his fingers. "If your blood pressure normalizes, if the swelling reduces significantly, and if Ryan drives you, then you can go. But don't plan on coming back to Missoula before delivery. Have the baby there in Whitefish. Your family doctor can handle it."

Tears spilled over before she could stop them. "Thank you. I'll spend the next few days taking care of myself, doing everything right. The baby has to come first. But I want her born surrounded by my family."

"I understand. Family is important, especially for a first baby. They'll want to be there for you."

"Yes," she managed, wiping at her tears with her free hand.

This was her wish. And Amelia always got what she wanted, well, usually. Eventually. Things were going to work out exactly like she'd planned, except better now, because Ryan would be there too.

"Where are you going to stay?" the doctor asked. "I heard all the hotels are full."

"With me," Ryan said immediately, looking at her for confirmation.

She really didn't have another choice. And honestly, it would give them time to talk, to figure out what this meant, to start planning for a future she'd given up hoping for.

"All right then," the doctor said. "Ryan, take good care of her. Put those feet up, rest, and have a Merry Christmas."

"Thank you," Amelia said, meaning it with everything in her.

After the doctor left, relief flooded through her so intensely she felt light-headed. Her baby was safe. Still nestled comfortably inside, not ready to arrive in the middle of a blizzard in a strange hospital.

Ryan helped her dress, and she couldn't help but laugh when his eyes went wide as he carefully pulled her maternity underwear up over her belly. The expression on his face, equal parts horrified and fascinated, was priceless.

"What about your Christmas party?" she asked as he helped her with her boots. "The children can't miss seeing Santa."

"No," he said firmly. "We need to get you home. Get you settled."

"Five minutes," she countered. "Just five minutes. Think of those children, they've been waiting for Santa. I'll sit in a corner and put my feet up, I promise. I don't want to disappoint them."

She could see him wavering, torn between his protective instincts and his commitment to the kids.

"Besides," she added, playing her trump card, "I'd like to see you in action as Santa. Our daughter should know her father is a hero who brings joy to sick children on Christmas."

His expression softened. "You're manipulating me."

"Is it working?"

"Unfortunately, yes." He sighed, but she could see the smile tugging at his lips. "All right. But five minutes only, and then we're leaving. And you're sitting down the entire time with your feet elevated."

"Deal," she said, grinning.

As they made their way back through the hospital corridors, Ryan still in his full Santa regalia, Amelia waddling along beside him, she marveled at how completely her life had changed in the span of a few hours.

This morning, she'd been alone, unemployed, pregnant, and terrified of telling her family.

Tonight, she had Ryan. The father of her baby. A man who'd searched for her as desperately as she'd searched for him. A man who looked at her like she was a gift instead of a problem.

Maybe the universe did have a plan after all.

Maybe getting stranded in a blizzard, having contractions in a hotel lobby, and finding Ryan dressed as Santa Claus was exactly what was supposed to happen.

She glanced up at him as they walked, at his strong profile and the determination in his eyes, and felt something settle in her chest. Something that felt dangerously close to hope.

"Hey, Ryan?"

"Yeah?"

"Thank you. For being so... for being here. For wanting this."

He stopped walking and turned to face her, right there

in the middle of the hospital corridor. His hand came up to cup her cheek, gentle and sure.

"Amelia, I spent nine months thinking I'd lost the best night of my life. Now I find out I'm going to be a father to your child?" His thumb brushed away a tear she hadn't realized had fallen. "I'm not going anywhere. We're in this together now."

Her throat tightened with emotion. "Together."

"Together," he confirmed. "Now let's go make some kids smile before I take you home and force-feed you vegetables and water until that blood pressure comes down."

She laughed, the sound surprising her with its genuine joy. "You really know how to sweet-talk a girl."

"Just wait until you see my Santa impression. You're going to be thoroughly charmed."

As they continued down the hall, Amelia felt lighter than she had in months. The road ahead was still uncertain, there were so many conversations to have, so many details to work out, and she still had to tell her family, but for the first time since she'd seen those two pink lines on the pregnancy test, she didn't feel alone.

And that made all the difference.

CHAPTER 7

The woman was going to be the death of him.

Amelia sat in that wheelchair looking up at him with those luminous eyes, her rounded belly resting between them like a promise, and Ryan knew he was completely, utterly done for. She was even more beautiful pregnant than she'd been that night on the cruise, fuller breasts, glowing skin, that serene Madonna quality women got when they were carrying life inside them.

All she had to do was tear up a little, bat those long lashes, and he'd do whatever she wanted.

The only problem? She knew it.

And she had a stubborn streak a mile wide.

He'd wanted to take her straight to his apartment, get her horizontal with her feet elevated above her heart, but no. She'd insisted they attend the Christmas party for the kids. Five minutes, she'd promised. Just five minutes to see Santa in action.

He was beginning to suspect those five minutes were going to stretch considerably longer.

Before they'd left the ER, he'd called Stan and Adam. They were already upstairs on the fifth floor, the pediatric oncology wing, waiting with the bag of toys they'd loaded into the ambulance hours ago. It felt like a lifetime had passed since then, though it had been less than two hours.

Two hours ago, he'd been Santa Claus heading to spread Christmas cheer.

Now he was Santa Claus about to become a father.

The elevator ride up felt interminable. Amelia sat quietly in the wheelchair, one hand resting on her belly, the other gripping the armrest. He'd positioned her feet as high as the footrests would allow, earning questioning looks from an orderly who'd gotten on at the third floor.

Let them look. Let them wonder.

Within an hour, everyone in this hospital would know that Ryan Allen had a pregnant girlfriend. The gossip network here was more efficient than any police scanner. But he didn't care. These people had his back. They'd supported him through the worst period of his life, had given him space when he needed it, and shown up when he didn't know how to ask for help.

They'd understand. Hell, they'd probably throw him a baby shower.

The elevator doors opened onto the fifth floor, and Ryan was immediately hit with the familiar mixture of antiseptic, hope, and heartbreak that defined this place. The nurses' station was lit up like a Christmas tree, literally. Garland wrapped around the desk, lights blinked in the windows, and someone had hung mistletoe above the medication cart.

Stan and Adam were there, flirting with the night shift nurses, all good women who laughed at their terrible jokes and flirted back because everyone needed a little lightness in a place where children fought for their lives.

These nurses were angels. They dealt with sick kids every single day, watched some of them deteriorate, held parents while they made impossible decisions, and still managed to smile. Still managed to make the children feel special, feel normal, feel loved.

Ryan couldn't imagine what they went through. Wouldn't want to.

The charge nurse, Bethany, a woman in her fifties with laugh lines around her eyes and iron in her spine, glanced up as he wheeled Amelia closer. Her gaze swept from the Santa suit to Amelia's belly to the protective way Ryan's hand rested on her shoulder.

Understanding dawned in her expression, followed by a smile that crinkled her whole face.

"The kids are waiting in the playroom," she said, pointing down the hall. "Room 512. Fair warning, we've got about fifteen tonight. Mix of outpatients and our long-term residents."

"Here's your bag of toys," Stan said, hefting the red velvet sack. He glanced at Amelia, then back at Ryan. "Nurse Brandon can push Amelia, and then we can get started."

Ryan hesitated. He didn't want to let go of the wheel-chair, didn't want to leave her even for the few minutes this would take. But one of the younger nurses, Brandon, a guy who'd started just six months ago, was already moving forward with an understanding smile.

"I've got her," Brandon said quietly. "We'll get her comfortable in the back of the room."

They moved down the hall quickly, Ryan's boots, still in full Santa regalia, squeaking slightly on the polished floor. He had to do this fast and then get Amelia home. But part of him was genuinely glad they weren't missing the party.

This tradition mattered to him. It kept his mind occupied during the hardest season of the year. It reminded him that even in the darkest times, there was still joy to be found, still light to share.

It kept him from drowning in memories of another little girl who should still be here.

Brandon wheeled Amelia into the playroom first, positioning her wheelchair in the back corner where she could watch but stay out of the chaos. Ryan waited outside with Stan and Adam, letting anticipation build.

Then they burst through the door.

"Ho, ho, ho! Merry Christmas!"

The room erupted. Kids who could jump did. Those in wheelchairs clapped. A little boy on a rolling IV pole started bouncing so hard his mother had to steady him. Even the sickest children, the ones in hospital beds that had been wheeled in for the occasion, managed smiles.

Ryan's heart expanded and broke simultaneously, the way it always did in this room.

He started with the healthier kids first, the ones who were here for minor surgeries or short-term treatments. A girl with a broken leg in a purple cast. Twin boys recovering from appendectomies. A teenager with a wrist injury who tried to look too cool for Santa but couldn't quite hide his grin when Ryan handed him a video game he'd been wanting.

But when he moved to the row of truly sick children, the ones with bald heads and hollow eyes and skin so pale it was nearly translucent, he slowed down. These kids deserved more than a quick handoff and a "ho ho ho."

He crouched beside the first bed, where a little boy who couldn't have been more than five lay propped against pillows. His mother sat beside him, holding his hand.

"Merry Christmas," Ryan said, keeping his voice gentle. "I'm praying that you receive healing and have a wonderful Christmas."

The boy's eyes lit up. "Did you really come from the North Pole?"

"I did. And you know what? The elves told me you've been very, very good this year."

"Even when I cried during the treatments?"

Ryan's chest tightened. "Especially then. Being brave doesn't mean you don't cry. It means you keep going even when things are hard."

The mother's eyes filled with tears. "Thank you," she whispered.

He moved to the next child, then the next. A girl who wanted to be a veterinarian. A boy who loved dinosaurs. Another girl who showed him the picture she'd drawn of her family.

When he reached a mother who looked like she hadn't slept in days, shoulders slumped, eyes rimmed with red, he didn't hesitate. He pulled her into a hug, feeling her shake against him.

"Thank you," she whispered near his ear. "You're a blessing."

"You're the blessing," he murmured back. "Your daughter is lucky to have you."

He made his way around the room, acutely aware of time passing, of Amelia watching from her wheelchair in the corner. He wanted to get her home, get her settled, but he couldn't rush this. These kids deserved his full attention.

Finally, he reached the last bed. A little girl with wise eyes and a smile that seemed too big for her small face looked up at him. She couldn't have been more than seven.

"Santa, thank you," she said, her voice soft but clear. "But you should give this toy to one of the other kids. I'm not going to be here much longer."

The words hit him like a physical blow. Tears sprang to his eyes before he could stop them. Across the bed, her mother looked away, quickly wiping at her own face.

Ryan swallowed hard, forcing himself to stay present, to not fall apart in front of this brave little girl.

"No, sweetie." He placed the wrapped present, a stuffed

unicorn with a sparkly horn, in her hands. "I want you to have this present. This one is specifically for you. And it doesn't matter how long you play with it. It's here for as long as you need it."

A grin spread across her face, genuine and delighted. "Merry Christmas, Santa."

His throat was so tight he could barely speak. "Merry Christmas, sweetheart. Giving you this present has made my Christmas even happier. You've given Santa a gift too, reminding me what courage looks like."

"Thank you," she whispered, already hugging the unicorn close.

He had to walk away before he completely lost his composure. As it was, he could feel tears threatening, and the girl's mother was openly crying now, trying to muffle the sound with her hand.

At the door, Ryan turned back. The room was full of noise now, kids playing with new toys, parents smiling, nurses moving between beds, adjusting IVs, and checking monitors. For this one moment, this room wasn't a place of illness and fear. It was just a place where children were being children, where Christmas magic was real.

"Ho, ho, ho!" he called out, his voice only slightly unsteady. "Merry Christmas to all, and to all a good night!"

The kids called back, their voices a chorus of joy and hope.

Then he stepped into the hallway and let the door close behind him.

His composure cracked immediately. He made it to the

nurses' station and grabbed a tissue, pressing it to his eyes before the tears could fall.

"Gets to you every time, doesn't it, Santa?" Bethany said gently. She'd seen him do this for two years now, had probably watched countless other Santas break down in this same spot.

"Yes." His voice was rough. "That little girl, the last one, what's wrong with her?"

Bethany's expression softened with sympathy. "You know I can't tell you specific diagnoses. HIPAA and all that. But..." She glanced around, then lowered her voice. "It starts with a C. Stage four. And no, she's not doing well. We'll be lucky if she's still here on New Year's Day."

The tissue crumpled in his fist. Cancer. Of course it was cancer.

Stan appeared beside him, pushing Amelia's wheelchair. His usually jovial expression was somber, haunted. Adam trailed behind, looking like a kicked puppy.

For the last two years, this had been their routine: hand out presents at the hospital, then head to Murphy's Bar where Stan and Adam would get thoroughly drunk while Ryan nursed a single beer and made sure they got home safely. It had seemed like the only appropriate response to what they witnessed in that room, the only way to process the unfairness of children suffering while they got to walk away healthy and whole.

But tonight felt different.

Tonight, Ryan had his own child to think about. A daughter growing inside Amelia, safe and healthy and wanted. How could he go to a bar and drink away his sorrow when he had so much to be grateful for?

"Thanks, Stan," Ryan said quietly. "I had to get out of there."

"I know." Stan's voice was thick. "That last kid..."

"Yeah."

Adam cleared his throat. "I'm assuming you're not joining us for drinks tonight. But I'm headed to the bar anyway. I'll call an Uber to get home."

Normally, Ryan would have protested. He was always the designated driver, the one who made sure his guys got home safe after they'd dealt with the heartbreak of this place. He'd have one drink to their five and drive them both home, making sure they didn't do something stupid in their grief.

But tonight, he had other responsibilities.

"I'm going with you," Stan said to Adam. "We can share the Uber. Be smart about it."

"Time for me to get Amelia home," Ryan said, his hand finding her shoulder again, grounding himself in her presence. "Either in bed or with her feet propped up."

"And food," Amelia interjected, looking up at him with a tired smile. "I need food. This baby likes to eat."

Despite everything, the dying children, the grief, the weight of the evening, Ryan felt a grin spread across his face. Life continued. His child was hungry. That mattered.

"I doubt many places are open in this storm, but I make a mean pizza. Do you like pizza?"

"Yes," she said, laughing. "But I am really tired."

"Veggie pizza," he clarified. "Because you don't need pepperoni. Too much grease, too much salt."

She gazed up at him, shaking her head with amused exasperation.

"I'm certain the next few days are going to be very interesting."

"I plan on taking very good care of you," he said, meaning every word.

Stan and Adam chuckled. "Sorry, Amelia," Stan said. "If you need something besides vegetables, send us a text. We'll bring you a big juicy hamburger."

"Oh." Amelia sighed longingly. "With french fries?"

"Extra crispy," Adam added.

Ryan shook his head. "You guys know better. A pregnant woman with high blood pressure needs to watch her sodium intake."

"And she needs to eat," Amelia countered. "She needs to not starve while—"

Her words cut off abruptly. She gasped, her hand flying to her belly, her whole body going rigid.

Guilt slammed into Ryan. He'd wasted too much time. She should already be at his apartment with her feet elevated and food in her stomach.

"Time to go, princess," he said, crouching beside the wheelchair, his hand covering hers on her belly. "You're still having Braxton Hicks. We need to get you horizontal."

The contraction lasted thirty seconds, he counted silently, watching her breathe through it. When her body finally relaxed, he stood and started pushing the wheelchair toward the elevator.

Stan and Adam followed, their earlier levity replaced with concern.

The elevator ride down was silent except for the mechanical hum and Amelia's slightly labored breathing. When the doors opened to the parking garage, cold air rushed in, making her shiver.

"If you need anything, anything at all, call," Stan said.

"You'll be drunk," Ryan pointed out.

"Nope. We'll keep our phones on. We've got your back, man."

Ryan nodded, grateful for friends who understood without needing explanation. "Have one for me. Stay safe."

"You too. Take care of your girl."

Your girl. The words settled into his chest, feeling right and terrifying and perfect all at once.

He wheeled Amelia through the garage to where he'd left his Jeep, Wrangler, that had seemed practical and fun when he'd bought it.

Now, looking at Amelia's exhausted face and very pregnant belly, it seemed like the worst possible vehicle choice.

She stared up at it, then looked at him incredulously. "How in the hell am I supposed to climb into that?"

He couldn't help it, he laughed. "I've got you."

Before she could protest, he slipped his arms around her, one under her knees, one supporting her back, and lifted her in one smooth motion. She was heavier than she'd been nine months ago, her center of gravity completely different, but he was strong enough. More than strong enough.

He settled her into the passenger seat, making sure she was secure, then leaned in close. She smelled like hospital soap and something floral, her shampoo, maybe, and underneath it all, something that was uniquely Amelia.

"Let's go home," he said softly. "Time for you to put your feet up and rest."

"Home," she repeated, and something in her voice made his chest ache.

She'd been alone for nine months. But she wasn't alone anymore.

He was going to make damn sure she never felt alone again.

CHAPTER 8

melia's hands twisted in her lap as Ryan's Jeep navigated through the thickening snow. The windshield wipers worked frantically, their rhythmic swoosh doing little to calm her racing heart. Nine months. It had been nine months since that night on the cruise ship, nine months since she'd felt his hands on her skin, heard his laugh in the darkness, tasted salt air and possibility on his lips.

What if it had all been an illusion? A perfect moment suspended in time that couldn't survive the harsh light of reality?

She stole a glance at his profile, illuminated by the dashboard lights. Strong jaw, focused eyes scanning the road ahead. He was even more handsome than she remembered, which seemed impossibly unfair. Meanwhile, she was roughly the size and shape of a beached whale.

Her hand drifted to her swollen belly, feeling the baby

shift beneath her palm. At least one good thing had come from that night. But Ryan... what must he think of her now?

Here she sat in his Jeep, enormous and ungainly, stretch marks mapping her abdomen like fault lines in the earth. Her breasts were heavy and tender, already preparing for their purpose, and she felt about as sexy as a barn.

"You're awfully quiet," Ryan said, his voice cutting through her spiral of anxiety.

"Just tired," she lied, watching the snow swirl hypnotically in the headlights.

"We're almost there." His hand reached across the console, hovering near hers for a moment before settling on the gearshift instead. Had he been about to touch her? The thought sent an unexpected flutter through her chest that had nothing to do with the baby.

They pulled up in front of a well-maintained brick building, its windows glowing warmly against the storm. Ryan's apartment complex looked solid, respectable, nothing like the cramped quarters some of her college boyfriends had inhabited. But then again, Ryan wasn't a college boyfriend. He wasn't a boyfriend at all. He was the father of her child, and she had no idea what that made them to each other.

"My suitcase," she said suddenly, remembering. "It's still in my car, and if this snow keeps up—"

"I'll get it," Ryan interrupted, already unbuckling his seatbelt. "Let me get you settled inside first, then I'll head back out."

"Ryan, it's getting dangerous out there." She gestured to the windshield, where snow was already accumulating despite the wipers' best efforts.

"My Jeep gets me through worse than this every winter. I'm not worried." He turned to face her fully, and something in his expression made her breath catch. "You're not going with me, though. You need to be off your feet."

"I can walk a few yards—"

"Amelia." Her name on his lips stopped her protest cold. "Let me take care of you. Please."

The vulnerability in those last words undid something in her chest. When was the last time someone had wanted to take care of her? She'd been so fiercely independent, so determined to handle everything alone. And look where it had gotten her, alone, pregnant, jobless, and stranded in a snowstorm.

"Okay," she whispered.

Relief washed over his features. "Sit tight. I'll unlock the door and come back for you."

She watched him sprint through the snow to the building's entrance, his broad shoulders hunched against the wind. The door swung open, spilling warm light onto the snowy sidewalk, and then he was running back to her. When he yanked open the passenger door, a gust of frigid air and snowflakes swirled into the Jeep.

"It's really coming down now," he said, brushing snow from his hair. "Ready?"

"Ryan, I'm too heavy. I can walk—"

"Would you stop arguing and wrap your arms around my neck?"

There was something almost desperate in his tone, as if taking care of her was something he needed to do, not just something he felt obligated to do. Slowly, she complied, linking her fingers behind his neck as he slid one arm beneath her knees and the other around her back.

He lifted her with surprising ease, as if she weighed nothing at all. "See? Not too heavy."

"You're just trying to be chivalrous," she muttered against his shoulder, but she couldn't suppress the small smile tugging at her lips. He smelled the same, clean soap and something indefinably masculine that made her want to bury her face in his neck.

The few yards to the door felt simultaneously too long and not long enough. Snow caught in her eyelashes and melted on her cheeks. Ryan's arms were steady around her, his heartbeat strong against her side. For the first time in months, she felt safe.

Inside, the warmth enveloped them like an embrace. Ryan carried her to a chocolate-brown loveseat and gently lowered her onto the cushions.

"This reclines," he explained, demonstrating with the lever on the side. "So you can elevate your feet. The remote's right here on the end table. Bathroom's down the hall, first door on the right."

Before she could respond, he was moving with purposeful efficiency, hanging up his coat, striding to the kitchen, returning with a glass of water and a bowl of grapes.

"Pregnant women are supposed to stay hydrated," he said, setting both items on the coffee table within easy reach. A faint flush colored his cheeks.

The man was a paramedic. A very good one, from what she could see. She didn't know what to say to that, so she simply watched as he grabbed his coat again and pulled a scrap of paper from his pocket, scribbling something quickly.

"My phone number," he said, pressing it into her hand. "Call me if you need anything, anything at all. If you go into labor, which I really don't think you will, call me immediately. I can be back here in under five minutes with lights and sirens if I have to."

"You're a paramedic, not an ambulance service."

"For you? I'll make an exception." He grinned, and for one breathless moment, she thought he might kiss her. Instead, he straightened, his expression turning serious. "I'll be back in thirty minutes, forty max. And Amelia? Don't try to do anything heroic while I'm gone. No cleaning, no cooking, no rearranging furniture. Just rest."

"Sir, yes, sir," she said with a mock salute.

His grin returned, softening the hard lines of worry around his eyes. Then he was gone, the door clicking shut behind him. She heard the lock engage and then his footsteps fading away.

Silence descended like a blanket.

Amelia sat very still, absorbing the quiet. It was the first time in hours, that she'd been truly alone with her thoughts. The constant motion had stopped. No more highway rushing beneath her tires, no more forced cheerfulness with gas station attendants, no more white-knuckling it through dangerous road conditions while her back ached and the baby kicked her ribs.

Just silence. And in that silence, the fear crept in.

What if she went into labor right now, alone in Ryan's apartment? The doctor had said she was fine to travel, but doctors had been wrong before. What if something happened to Ryan on his way to her car? What if he couldn't find it in the storm, or worse, what if he slid off the road and—

Stop it, she told herself firmly. Ryan knew these roads. He drove an ambulance through worse conditions than this every day. He would be fine.

But the anxiety wouldn't quite release its grip on her heart.

With effort, she pushed herself up from the loveseat and began to explore the apartment. It was surprisingly spacious for a one-bedroom, with an open-concept living area that flowed into a small but functional kitchen. Everything was clean and organized, no dirty dishes in the sink, no laundry draped over furniture, no mysterious odors emanating from forgotten takeout containers. Ryan was naturally neat.

She ran her fingers along the back of the sofa, examining the space with the curiosity of someone trying to understand the man who lived here. A small bookshelf held an eclectic mix of thriller novels, medical texts, and, surprisingly, a collection of cooking magazines. The walls were decorated with framed prints of Montana landscapes, mountains at sunrise, rivers cutting through valleys, forests thick with pine.

Down the hallway, she found the bathroom Ryan had mentioned. It was just as meticulously kept as the rest of the apartment, with fresh towels folded on a shelf and toiletries lined up neatly on the counter. She used the facilities, the eternal curse of pregnancy, and washed her hands, studying her reflection in the mirror.

She looked exhausted. Dark circles shadowed her eyes, and her hair had frizzed in the humidity of the storm. Her face was rounder than it had been nine months ago, her features softer. She barely recognized herself.

Who was she now? Not the carefree woman who'd boarded that cruise ship, certainly. Not the successful professional she'd worked so hard to become, that person had been fired, her reputation tarnished by the very pregnancy she'd tried so hard to hide. She was in limbo, caught between who she'd been and who she was becoming.

And Ryan... where did he fit into this new version of herself?

As she emerged from the bathroom, a framed photograph on the hallway wall caught her attention. A beautiful woman with emerald eyes stood laughing at the camera, a toddler balanced on her hip. The little girl had wild curls and a gap-toothed grin, her chubby hands reaching for the camera.

Back in the living room, Amelia settled onto the loveseat again, this time activating the recliner function. Her swollen feet elevated, she released a sigh of relief. She hadn't realized how much they'd been aching until the pressure eased.

The apartment was warm and quiet, insulated from the storm raging outside. Through the window, she could see snow falling in thick curtains, already accumulating on the sill. She would never have made it to Whitefish in her little SUV. The thought of being stranded on some dark highway, alone and in labor, sent a shiver down her spine.

Thank God for Ryan. Thank God he'd been working today, that he'd been the one to respond to her call. What were the odds?

But now what? The question she'd been avoiding all day finally demanded attention. She was here, in Ryan's apartment, pregnant with his child. There was no more hiding, no more pretending she could handle everything alone.

They needed to talk. Really talk, about the baby and the future and what they meant to each other. Was it just that one perfect night? A fleeting connection that couldn't survive the weight of real-world consequences? Or was there something deeper, something worth fighting for?

She wanted there to be. God, she wanted that more than she'd let herself admit.

But what if he didn't? What if he was being kind because he was a good person, not because he felt anything for her beyond basic human decency and parental obligation? What if, once the baby was born, he faded back into his life while she returned to hers, and they became nothing more than co-parents coordinating drop-offs and holidays?

Her phone buzzed in her purse, startling her from her thoughts. She fished it out and saw three missed calls from her mother. Guilt washed over her. Of course her parents were worried sick.

She dialed her mother's number, listening to it ring once, twice—

"Amelia! Oh, thank God. Where are you? Are you safe?"

"Mom, yes, I'm fine. I'm stuck in Missoula. The roads to Whitefish are closed."

"Stuck? Oh, dear. Did you find a place to stay? Please tell me you're not in your car—"

"No, I'm fine. I've got a place to stay." The lie of omission tasted bitter on her tongue, but how could she explain Ryan over a phone call? How could she admit to nine months of secrecy in one breath?

Her mother's voice crackled with static. The connection was deteriorating. "Amelia, are you—danger—baby—"

"Mom? Mom, can you hear me?"

"—worried sick—roads are terrible here too—" The words cut in and out, fragmenting. "—be careful—love you—"

"I love you too, Mom. I'll call when I can get through, okay? Tell Dad not to worry."

But her mother couldn't hear her. The line dissolved into static and then silence. Amelia stared at her phone, watching the signal bars fluctuate weakly before disappearing entirely.

No service.

She was truly cut off now, isolated in this apartment with Ryan. The thought should have frightened her, but instead, it brought an odd sense of calm. For once, she didn't have to answer to anyone. There were no expectations to meet, no image to maintain, no careful explanations to craft. It was just her and Ryan and the truth between them.

When had her life become so complicated? She'd always been the golden child, the one who excelled at everything, whose plans unfolded exactly as designed. College honors, dream job, carefully mapped five-year plan. And then one impulsive week on a cruise ship had upended everything.

No, that wasn't fair. The baby wasn't a mistake, no matter how unplanned. This little person somersaulting inside her was a gift, even if the timing was terrible.

And Ryan... what was he?

The memory of that night flooded back unbidden, as vivid as if it were happening now. The way he'd looked at her on the ship's deck, moonlight painting silver highlights in his hair. The warmth of his hand finding hers as they'd talked. The moment when talking hadn't been enough anymore, when they'd stumbled back to his cabin, breathless with laughter and want.

It had been perfect. He had been perfect. Gentle and passionate, attentive and playful. She'd never felt so seen, so desired, so completely herself with another person.

But one night didn't make a relationship. One night didn't guarantee compatibility or shared values or a future together. One night was just that, a beautiful, isolated moment that might not translate to the messy reality of raising a child together.

Her eyes grew heavy as exhaustion finally caught up with her. The loveseat was surprisingly comfortable, cradling her aching body. Outside, the storm raged on, but in here, she was warm and safe. Ryan would be back soon. They would talk. They would figure this out.

She let her eyes drift closed, just for a moment.

Just for a moment...

CHAPTER 9

The roads were absolute hell.

Ryan gripped the steering wheel tighter as his Jeep fishtailed slightly on a patch of black ice. He corrected automatically, years of driving in Montana winters making the adjustment instinctive. But his jaw was clenched so hard it ached, and fury simmered beneath his careful focus.

What had Amelia been thinking? Nine months pregnant, driving alone through a blizzard to get to Whitefish for Christmas. She could have gone into labor on some desolate stretch of highway. She could have slid off the road, trapped in her car with the temperature dropping and no help for miles. The baby, their baby, could have been born in the freezing cold while Amelia bled out waiting for an ambulance that might not reach her in time.

He'd seen it happen. He'd responded to calls like that. The outcomes weren't always good.

His hands tightened on the wheel until his knuckles went white. He forced himself to breathe, to unclench his jaw. She was safe now. That was what mattered. She was in his apartment, warm and dry, with her feet elevated like they should be. He'd make sure she stayed that way.

But God, the thought of losing her, of losing them both before he'd even had a chance—

A car sat nose-down in the ditch ahead, hazard lights blinking weakly through the snow. Ryan's training kicked in, overriding his urgency to get back to Amelia. He pulled over, emergency flashers on, and approached the vehicle.

Twenty minutes later, he'd helped extract a terrified college kid and his girlfriend from their Honda Civic. The kid's hands had been shaking so badly Ryan had to call the tow truck for him. Another fifteen minutes down the road, he stopped again, this time for a family of four whose minivan had slid sideways into a snowbank. The kids were crying, the mother was on the verge of panic, and the father looked like he was about to have a heart attack.

Ryan helped them push the van back onto the road, gave them some advice about getting to the nearest hotel, and sent them on their way with a wave. His paramedic instincts wouldn't let him drive past someone in trouble, but each delay made his chest tighter with the need to get back to Amelia.

What if she went into labor while he was gone? What if something went wrong? The doctor had cleared her to travel, but doctors had been wrong before. He'd seen plenty of women deliver early, especially under stress. And if today hadn't been stressful, he didn't know what was.

Finally, with Amelia's suitcase secured in the back of his Jeep, he made one more stop, the grocery store. The parking lot was nearly empty; most sensible people had already hunkered down at home. Inside, he moved quickly through the aisles, grabbing items almost at random. Fresh fruit, grapes, strawberries, apples. Vegetables she could snack on. A prepared pizza because he sure as hell wasn't going to make her wait while he cooked from scratch.

He paused in the floral section, staring at the small selection of bouquets. When was the last time he'd bought flowers for a woman? Maybe never. Definitely not since—

He pushed that thought away and grabbed a mixed arrangement of pink and white roses. They reminded him of her, somehow. Soft and beautiful and perfect.

At the checkout, the teenage cashier gave him a knowing smile. "Someone's gonna have a good night."

"I hope so," Ryan said, and meant it more than the kid could possibly understand.

Back in the Jeep, he navigated the final stretch to his apartment, his mind churning. What was he going to say to her? How did you have a conversation about the rest of your lives when you'd only spent one night together nine months ago?

But what a night it had been.

He could still remember every detail. The way she'd laughed at his terrible jokes on the ship's deck, her head thrown back and her eyes sparkling in the moonlight. The way she'd looked at him like he was the only person in the world who mattered. The way she'd felt in his arms, soft and warm and right in a way nothing had felt right in years.

He'd known, even then, that she was special. That losing her phone number had been one of the biggest mistakes of his life.

And now she was here, carrying his child, and he'd be damned if he was going to let her slip away again.

The question was: what did Amelia want?

She'd seemed tense earlier, uncertain. Maybe she was just nervous about how he'd react to the pregnancy. Or maybe she didn't feel the same connection he did. Maybe that night had been just a vacation fling for her, a pleasant memory she'd planned to keep locked away until circumstances forced her hand.

The thought made his chest ache.

No. He couldn't think like that. She'd tried to find him. She'd called the cruise line. She hadn't kept the pregnancy a secret out of malice, she simply hadn't known how to reach him. Just like he hadn't known how to reach her, despite spending months searching every online directory he could find.

They'd both made mistakes. But they had a second chance now, and Ryan wasn't going to waste it.

His apartment building came into view, the windows glowing warmly against the storm. Through the blinds of his unit, he could see the flicker of the television. Good. Hopefully, she'd stayed put, resting like she needed to.

He parked and stepped out into snow that now reached his knees. It was still coming down hard, showing no signs of stopping. They'd be snowed in for at least a day, maybe two. Which meant time, time to talk, to figure things out, to see if what they'd had that one night could translate into something more.

He grabbed the groceries and her suitcase, shouldering his way through the snow to the building entrance. Inside, he stomped the worst of it off his boots.

Before he'd left to get her suitcase, he'd called his captain and requested time off. But his friends at the station had beaten him to it, apparently, they'd already cleared his schedule for the next week, volunteering to cover his shifts. Mike had texted him: *Take care of your girl. We've got you covered.*

His girl. God, he wanted that to be true.

Ryan unlocked the door and stepped inside. Amelia was curled up in the recliner, her eyes closed and her breathing deep and even. Asleep. Something in his chest loosened at the sight of her, safe and peaceful in his home.

He tried to be quiet, but the rustle of grocery bags gave him away. Her eyes fluttered open, confusion clouding them for a moment before recognition set in.

"You're back," she said, her voice still husky with sleep.

"Sorry it took so long." He set the bags down and held up the flowers. "I had to pull two families out of ditches, and then I stopped at the grocery store to stock up on things I thought you could eat. And I brought you these. I'm just, I'm so happy we found each other again."

Her expression softened in a way that made his heart skip. "Oh, thank you. I'd get up and put them in a vase, but I don't know if you have one."

"I'll take care of them," he said quickly. "You stay right there. After you doing this alone for nine months, bringing you flowers is literally the least I could do."

A genuine smile curved her lips, and Ryan felt like he'd won something important. "Thank you. I called my mother and told her I was stuck in Missoula."

"Good. That way she won't worry." He carried her suitcase toward the bedroom, then paused. "Are you hungry?"

"Starving."

"I picked up a pizza, no pepperoni. It'll just take a few minutes to heat up."

In the kitchen, he put away the groceries with automatic efficiency, his mind elsewhere. He found an old glass vase in the back of a cabinet, a relic from before, when his life had been different, and arranged the flowers as best he could. They looked better than he'd expected, actually. He set them on the coffee table where Amelia could see them.

Her suitcase went into his bedroom. He stood in the doorway for a moment, looking at his bed. It was neatly made, the dark blue comforter smooth and undisturbed. He tried to imagine Amelia there, her hair spread across his pillow, and the image sent heat spiraling through him.

But he couldn't push. Wouldn't push. Whatever happened between them had to be her choice too.

When he returned to the living room, Amelia was

struggling to her feet. "I was going to sleep here in the recliner," she said.

"Absolutely not. You're taking the bed." His tone left no room for argument. "I'll take the loveseat or the couch. I've slept on both plenty of times."

More than he cared to admit, actually. After the accident, he'd spent months avoiding his bedroom, unable to face the empty space. But that was a conversation for another day.

Amelia shuffled into the kitchen, one hand supporting her lower back. "Why are you being so nice to me?"

The question stopped him cold. He turned to face her fully, struck by the vulnerability in her eyes. "Because you deserve someone to treat you nice. And you're expecting my baby." He paused, then added more softly, "And because I haven't been able to stop thinking about you since that night."

Her breath caught audibly.

He busied himself with the pizza, removing the cellophane wrapper and sliding it into the preheated oven. "Fifteen minutes and we can eat."

"We need to talk," Amelia said, lowering herself carefully into one of his kitchen chairs.

"Yes." Ryan pulled out the chair across from her and sat down, his long legs barely fitting under the small table. "Are you up to it tonight?"

"I think so." She took a deep breath, her hands folding protectively over her belly. "Are you angry with me?"

God, was that what she thought? That he was angry?

"I was hurt," he said honestly. "When I woke up that morning and you were gone. When I realized you hadn't left me your phone number, any way to contact you. And then when I spent months searching for you and coming up empty." He ran a hand through his hair, trying to find the right words. "I even looked at every lawyer's website in Cheyenne, searching for anyone named Amelia. I must have looked at hundreds of profile photos, hoping I'd see your face."

Tears welled in her eyes. "I should have left you my number. But I woke up late, I had thirty minutes to pack and get up on deck before the ship docked. I was panicked and stupid, and I've regretted it every single day since." Her voice cracked. "And when I found out I was pregnant, I tried to find you. I really did. I contacted the cruise line, but they said they couldn't give out passenger information. I didn't know what else to do."

Ryan reached across the table and took her hand. Her fingers were small and cold in his, and he squeezed gently. "We both made mistakes. But we found each other again. That's what matters now."

"Yes," she whispered, her eyes fixed on their joined hands. "Now we're having a baby."

"A baby." The word still felt surreal, impossible. He was going to be a father. "I know we just found each other again. And I know this is complicated. But can we try?" The words tumbled out, propelled by the fear that she might say no. "Can we get to know each other, see if what we had that night is worth pursuing? See if there's a future for us?"

Even as he asked, he knew his answer. He'd marry her tomorrow if she'd have him. Tonight, if he could arrange it. He'd do whatever it took to make this work, to build the family he'd thought he'd never have again.

A slow smile spread across Amelia's face, and the warmth in her eyes nearly undid him. "Yes. I'd like that very much." She squeezed his hand. "Regardless of what happens between us, you'll always be this baby's father. And I'll share her with you."

"Her?" The word hit him like a physical blow. "It's a girl?"

Pain lanced through his chest, sharp and unexpected and completely irrational. He wasn't disappointed. How could he be disappointed? A healthy baby was all that mattered. But a girl. A daughter. Images he'd thought he'd buried forever clawed their way to the surface: wild curls and a gap-toothed grin, sticky hands reaching for him, laughter like music.

He pushed the memories down brutally. This was different. This was his and Amelia's daughter. A new life, a new chance. The past didn't have to define the future.

"Yes," Amelia said softly, watching him with concern. "Is that... is that okay?"

Ryan forced the pain away and looked at her, really looked at her. The woman carrying his daughter. The woman who made him laugh and think and feel more alive than he had in years. "It's more than okay. It's perfect."

Her smile widened with relief.

"Although," he said, trying to lighten the moment, "I've already discovered one thing about you."

"Oh?" Her eyebrows rose. "What's that?"

"You have a stubborn streak a mile wide."

He held his breath, hoping she wouldn't take offense. But instead, she laughed, that same uninhibited laugh he remembered from the cruise ship. "I'm not stubborn. I just know what I want, and most of the time, I get it." Her expression dimmed slightly. "Though I'll admit, these last few months haven't been great."

"Why not?"

She sighed, looking down at their still-joined hands. "The reason you couldn't find me on any lawyer's website is because I was fired. They claimed my work wasn't up to their standards, but we both know that's garbage. My work is excellent, I graduated at the top of my class. But they were a bunch of conservative old men who didn't want an unmarried pregnant woman working for them. What an embarrassment to the firm, right?"

Anger flared hot in Ryan's chest. "Those bastards."

"Exactly." A fierce light entered her eyes. "But you know what? I'm a damn good lawyer. Top of my class, like I said. So they can kiss my very large pregnant ass."

Ryan burst out laughing. This, this was what had drawn him to her that first night on the cruise. Her fire, her confidence, her refusal to let anyone diminish her. That hadn't changed. If anything, she burned brighter now.

The oven timer dinged, cutting through his laughter.

"Thank God," Amelia said dramatically. "This baby is demanding food."

Ryan stood and leaned down, unable to resist any longer. He pressed a gentle kiss to the tip of her nose, chaste and sweet and full of promise. Her eyes widened, her lips parting slightly.

"Go get back in the recliner," he said, his voice rougher than intended. "I'll bring your food to you."

She rose slowly, holding his gaze. "I could get used to you taking care of me."

And that, Ryan thought as she shuffled back toward the living room, was exactly what he wanted to hear. He pulled the pizza from the oven, his hands steady despite the emotions churning in his chest.

This was just the beginning. They had so much to figure out, where they'd live, how they'd co-parent, whether what they felt for each other was real or just the remnants of one perfect night. But for the first time since he'd lost everything two years ago, Ryan felt something he'd thought was gone forever.

Hope.

CHAPTER 10

$\mathcal{A}$melia's bladder woke her at six thirty, insistent and unforgiving. She lay there for a moment in Ryan's guest bedroom, staring at the unfamiliar ceiling, trying to orient herself. The sheets smelled like fabric softener and something masculine, not cologne, just clean and male. The room was cold enough that she could see her breath, but under the heavy comforter, she was warm. Safe.

Pregnant and stranded in a blizzard with the father of her baby.

If someone had told her twenty-four hours ago that this was how her life would unfold, she would have laughed in their face.

She pushed herself upright, no easy feat with forty extra pounds and a belly that seemed to have its own gravitational pull, and waddled to the bathroom. Through the window, she could see snow still falling in thick, relentless sheets. It had piled up against the side of the building, drifts reaching nearly four feet high. The parking lot below was buried, cars transformed into anonymous white lumps.

They weren't going anywhere today. Maybe not tomorrow either.

Part of her wanted to panic about that, about missing Christmas with her family, about her mother's disappointment, about the secret she still had to reveal. But another part of her, a part she was just beginning to acknowledge, felt relieved. Here, in this cocoon of snow and silence, she could pretend the outside world didn't exist. She could just be Amelia and Ryan, figuring out how to be parents together without the weight of everyone else's expectations.

After using the bathroom, for the third time since midnight, she pulled on the maternity sweats she'd packed and a large cream-colored sweater that stretched over her belly but didn't quite hide it. Nothing hid it anymore. She felt like a waddling cow, all swollen ankles and ungainly movements. How Ryan could look at her and call her beautiful was beyond her comprehension.

The smell of coffee drew her out of the bedroom like a siren's call. She followed it down the short hallway, her hand trailing along the wall for balance, and found Ryan in the kitchen.

Her breath caught.

He stood at the counter in grey sweatpants that hung low on his hips and nothing else, his back to her as he measured coffee grounds. His shoulders were broad, muscles defined under smooth skin, and his hair stuck up in several directions like he'd just rolled out of bed. Which he probably had.

God, he was beautiful. All lean muscle and masculine grace, and for one night, one perfect, reckless night, he'd been hers.

The memory hit her with unexpected force. His hands on her skin. His mouth against her neck. The way he'd looked at her like she was the only woman in the world. They'd barely made it into his cruise ship suite before they were tearing at each other's clothes, nine months of pent-up attraction exploding between them. She'd had more orgasms that night than in the previous year combined.

And somewhere during all that passion, during one of those frantic, desperate moments, something had gone wrong with the condom. One determined little swimmer had made it through, and now here they were.

She should regret it. Should wish it hadn't happened.

But she didn't. Not even a little bit.

He turned and saw her standing there, and his face lit up with a smile that made her heart skip. "Good morning."

"Good morning," she managed, suddenly feeling shy. "Is the coffee ready?"

"Just finished brewing." He reached for a mug. "What do you like in it?"

"Cream and sugar."

"How are you feeling this morning?"

She thought about lying, about saying she felt fine. But

there was something about Ryan that made her want to be honest, even when the truth wasn't pretty.

"Like a beached whale," she admitted, moving closer to the kitchen counter. "But no more Braxton Hicks, and my feet aren't as swollen as yesterday."

"Good." He doctored her coffee exactly how she liked it, then handed it to her, his fingers brushing hers in a way that sent electricity up her arm. "That's what I wanted to hear."

They moved to the small kitchen table, a simple wood affair with two chairs that looked out onto the snow-covered balcony. Amelia lowered herself carefully into one chair while Ryan took the other.

Automatically, without seeming to think about it, his hand reached across the table and covered hers.

The touch was casual, intimate, familiar in a way that shouldn't have been possible after only one night together nine months ago. But somehow it was. His palm was warm against her knuckles, his thumb tracing small circles on her skin that made her breath catch.

She hadn't been touched like this in so long. Hadn't been kissed, hadn't been held, hadn't felt desired. For months, she'd been pregnant and alone, an object of pity or judgment but never want.

"I'm glad you're here," Ryan said quietly.

The words hung between them, heavy with meaning.

"Even though I'm fat and pregnant?" The question came out more vulnerable than she'd intended.

"You're beautiful." His voice was firm, certain. "You

were beautiful when I met you, and now you have that glow pregnant women get. Honey, you're perfect."

She wanted to believe him. Wanted to accept the compliment at face value. But months of feeling unattractive, of watching men's eyes slide past her without interest, of catching her reflection and seeing only the weight she'd gained, made it impossible.

"You're just being nice," she said, looking down at her coffee. "I've gained forty pounds. The baby only weighs about five pounds right now. The rest has settled in my stomach and my ass."

Ryan's fingers squeezed hers, demanding her attention. When she looked up, his expression was so sincere it made her throat tight.

"No, I'm not just being nice. You're beautiful, and you're carrying my child. That makes you even more beautiful to me." He paused, his green eyes holding hers. "You'll lose the weight after the baby comes if you want to. But right now, you're exactly as you should be. You're creating life, Amelia. That's not something to apologize for."

Tears pricked at her eyes. Damn hormones. "Two weeks from now she should arrive. Right after the first of the year. Though if I had my way, it would be as soon as I get to Whitefish."

"Tell me about Whitefish," Ryan said. "Who lives there?"

"My parents. My sisters will be there for Christmas." She took a sip of coffee, letting the warmth spread through her chest. "I haven't told them I'm pregnant yet. They're going to be shocked."

That was an understatement. Her parents would be stunned. Disappointed, maybe, that she hadn't done things the "right" way. But they'd love her through it. They always did.

"Why haven't you told them?" Ryan asked gently.

The question opened something in her chest, something she'd been holding tight for months.

"I tried," she admitted. "Back in the beginning, around twelve weeks, I called my mom with every intention of telling her. But she was crying when she answered. Something was wrong, she never told me what, and I couldn't add to whatever she was dealing with. I couldn't say, 'Oh, by the way, I'm pregnant and I can't find the father.'"

Ryan flinched slightly at that, but she pressed on.

"And then in November, she made this odd request. She wanted all of us to come home for Christmas. Not just visit, really come home, like it was important. Urgent, even. That's the only reason I agreed to travel this close to my due date. Otherwise, I would have stayed in Cheyenne." She met his eyes. "But I want my mother by my side when I have this baby. I want my family there. And now I want you there too."

"Really?" His voice was careful, like he was afraid of her answer.

"Of course." The words came out fierce, certain. "I wouldn't want anyone else."

"I'll be your coach," he said immediately. "I'll be there for everything."

The tears came then, spilling over before she could stop

them. She'd spent so many nights lying awake, terrified of going through labor alone. Terrified of being in that delivery room with only nurses who didn't know her, who couldn't hold her hand and tell her everything would be okay.

"But what if I can't do this?" The fear bubbled up, overwhelming. "What if I'm screaming and begging and crying and I can't push her out and something goes wrong and—"

Ryan lifted her hand to his mouth and pressed a kiss to her knuckles, stopping her spiral. "I'll be there to calm you down. We can do this. Together."

"That's easy for you to say." She tried to pull herself together, swiping at her tears with her free hand. "You won't be the one pushing a seven-pound baby out through your vagina."

A smile filled his face, spreading all the way to his eyes, crinkling the corners in a way that made him even more attractive. The man was seriously excited about this child. Not just accepting it, not just resigned to it, but genuinely thrilled.

"No," he agreed, "but together we can do this. I'll be there encouraging you, giving you ice chips, telling you to breathe. And I can't wait to meet this sweet child we created."

Something in her chest loosened. His touch, his voice, the steady certainty in his eyes, it was like a balm to wounds she hadn't even known she was carrying. For months, she'd felt broken, wrong, like she'd made a mistake that couldn't be fixed. But Ryan made her feel like maybe this was exactly what was supposed to happen. Like their baby wasn't a mistake at all, but a gift.

"Ryan, I know we were just a one-night stand—"

"Hush," he interrupted, his thumb still tracing patterns on her hand. "We could have been so much more if we hadn't been so stupid. I should have gotten your last name and phone number before we ever had sex. Hell, I should have gotten them before we even got on the elevator. When I woke up and you were gone..." His jaw tightened. "I panicked. I ran up and down that hallway in my sweats like a crazy person."

The image made her smile despite her tears. "I had an early departure. I woke up late and didn't even think to leave a note. I regretted it later."

"Any note would have been better than nothing." His voice was soft, not accusatory. "But we both messed up. We're here now. That's what matters."

She nodded, wondering how different their lives would have been if they'd exchanged numbers. Would they be together now? Would they have been dating these last nine months, going to doctors' appointments together, picking out baby names over dinner?

"Tell me about yourself," she said, needing to know more, to understand the man who'd given her this child. "I know so little. Just that you're a paramedic who looks devastating in a Santa suit."

He laughed, the sound warm and genuine. "I'm the oldest of four boys. Clint is a couple of years younger than me, he works at the hospital as a nurse, actually. My two younger brothers, Mason and Tyler, are still in college. Pre-med and engineering, respectively." He paused. "My parents are retired and live here in Missoula. I grew up here, and I love it. Big enough to have everything you need, small enough to still feel like a community. I'd like to stay here and raise a family."

The words settled into her chest, both comforting and complicated. He wanted to stay in Missoula. She'd been planning to move back to Whitefish, to be near her family, to start over somewhere she was known and loved.

"Sounds like a nice place to grow up," she said carefully. "Whitefish is smaller. Maybe nine thousand people. Very much a resort town."

"I'd love to introduce you to my family," Ryan said. "But we're not getting out in this weather. And honestly, I don't want you risking a fall. All it would take is one slip on the ice, and that baby would decide to make an early entrance."

"I'd love to meet your family, too. See which parent you look like, meet your brothers." She smiled. "Are any of them married?"

"No. It's my mother's greatest disappointment that none of us have settled down and given her grandchildren." His grin turned wicked. "Guess she'll be over the moon when she learns about the baby. I'll be the golden child for once."

"Golden child." Amelia grimaced. "My sisters call me that. They hate it."

"Why?"

"Because I've always been the one who did everything right. Valedictorian in high school. Head cheerleader. Top of my class in law school. I got the prestigious job. I was perfect." She looked down at her belly. "And then I had my imperfect year."

"Tell me about your family," Ryan said gently. "What are they like?"

The question opened a floodgate. She told him about her parents, her father's gruff exterior that hid a marshmallow heart, her mother's quiet strength. About Emma, her twin, who was so different from her it was hard to believe they'd shared a womb. Emma was a NICU nurse studying to become a physician's assistant. Olivia, the chaos agent, had spent the last decade ricocheting from one disaster to another.

"They're going to lose their minds when they see me," Amelia said. "But they'll love me through it. That's what we do."

"Sounds like my family," Ryan said.

They sat in comfortable silence for a moment, just looking at each other across the small table. Outside, the snow continued to fall. Inside, something was building between them, something that felt bigger than just co-parenting, bigger than just attraction.

"Can I ask you something?" Ryan's voice was careful. "When you found out you were pregnant... why didn't you get an abortion? Most women in your situation would have at least considered it."

The question should have offended her. Should have felt like an accusation. But the genuine curiosity in his eyes told her he was really asking, really trying to understand.

Was he trying to figure out if she'd kept the baby to trap him? To see if she'd had other options?

"Every woman has a choice," she said slowly, "and mine was to have this baby. I've called her my little accident for eight months, and I love her with all my heart. From the moment I saw those two pink lines, even though I was terrified, even though I had no idea how I was going to do it alone... I knew I wanted her."

The words came out fierce, protective. This baby was hers. No one got to question that.

Ryan's face transformed. His smile was incandescent as he stood and came around the table. Before she could ask what he was doing, he was lifting her from the chair, no easy feat given her size, and wrapping his arms around her as far as they would reach around her belly.

"Thank you," he said against her hair. "I'm so happy. I can't wait to meet her. Can't wait to be her father."

And then his mouth was descending, covering hers, and it was like coming home.

She'd kissed him nine months ago in a frenzy of desire and whiskey courage. But this kiss was different. Slower. Sweeter. Filled with promise instead of just passion.

Her arms reached up and wrapped around his neck, pulling him closer. There was something about Ryan that drew her to him like a magnet, something that made her feel safe and wanted and cherished.

When they broke apart, both breathing hard, he smiled down at her with such tenderness it made her chest ache.

"How about I fix you some eggs?" he asked. "Are you hungry?"

She laughed, the sound lighter than she'd felt in months. "Am I pregnant? Yes, I'm starving."

"Good," he said, his hand finding her belly, spreading wide across the swell where their daughter grew. "Let's feed you both."

And standing there in his kitchen, snow falling outside, his arms around her and their baby between them, Amelia felt something she hadn't felt in a very long time.

She felt like maybe, just maybe, everything was going to be okay.

CHAPTER 11

After breakfast, Ryan cleaned up the dishes while Amelia settled into the living room. He could hear her moving around, the soft grunt as she lowered herself onto the loveseat, the sigh when she finally got her feet elevated. Every sound made him hyperaware of her presence in his space, filling it in a way no one had since Sandy died.

He made them a large salad, enough to last a few days, using the vegetables he'd stocked up on before the storm hit. Then he started a pot of homemade vegetable soup, the kind his mother used to make when he was sick as a kid. Being homemade meant he could control the sodium, could use herbs and spices instead of salt. Amelia's blood pressure had to come down if she wanted any hope of getting to Whitefish.

Not that he was particularly eager to let her go.

When the soup was simmering and the kitchen was

clean, he found her on the loveseat recliner, her feet propped up, scrolling through her phone with intense concentration. He sank down beside her, close enough that their thighs touched.

"What are you doing?" he asked.

"I'm googling Braxton Hicks and what to expect in the last days of pregnancy." She didn't look up from her screen. "This site has had a great list of things to expect every month. I'm so ready for this baby to come, but I still want her to wait until we reach Whitefish."

There it was again. Whitefish. Like a mantra she kept repeating, reminding him that she had a plan and he wasn't part of it. Not originally, anyway.

He looked over her shoulder at the article she was reading. "Here's a list of things to do to encourage the baby to come. Exercise and walking."

Right on cue, the wind slammed against the balcony door with enough force to rattle the frame. Snow pelted the glass like tiny bullets. Ryan glanced toward the window and sighed.

"I don't think walking is going to happen today. Not with this storm raging outside."

He'd been in this apartment for a year now, and it had served its purpose, a place to sleep, a place to escape the memories that haunted the house he'd shared with Sandy and Emma. But it was just an apartment. Someday, he wanted to move into a real house again. A place with a yard where kids could play, where he could teach his daughter to ride a bike, where there was room to grow.

The old house had been full of ghosts. He'd hear Sandy's voice calling to him from the kitchen, or Emma's laughter echoing down the hallway, and it would gut him all over again. Selling it had been the right choice, even if it had felt like betrayal at the time.

"Spicy food or castor oil," he read from Amelia's screen, pulling himself back to the present.

She wrinkled her nose. "Spicy food, yes. But castor oil? Just yuck. I'd have to be really desperate to try that stuff."

Good. The baby needed to stay put for as long as possible. The last thing he wanted was for her to try inducing labor, especially when they were trapped here by the storm. There was no way they were getting to Whitefish until the blizzard passed. Maybe not even then.

Maybe not until after the baby was born.

He knew he should let her go. Knew she wanted to be with her family, wanted her mother by her side. But part of him, a selfish, terrified part, wanted her to stay right here where he could keep her safe.

Amelia started to giggle, the sound surprising him.

"What?"

"Sex!" She looked up at him, her eyes dancing with amusement. "Look, it says sex can induce labor. Semen contains prostaglandins, which can soften the cervix. And an orgasm stimulates the uterus and releases oxytocin, which causes contractions."

Ryan's entire body went rigid. Heat flooded through him so fast he felt light-headed.

Did she have any idea what she was doing to him?

Sitting there talking so casually about orgasms and sex while her body was pressed against his, while he could smell her shampoo and feel the warmth of her skin through her clothes?

He would pick her up and carry her to the bedroom right now if she gave him even the slightest indication that's what she wanted. Their night together had been mind-blowing, the kind of chemistry that only happens once in a lifetime. He'd spent nine months remembering the taste of her skin, the sounds she made, the way her body had responded to his touch.

But this wasn't the time. She was nine months pregnant, exhausted from traveling, and dealing with high blood pressure. He wouldn't push. Couldn't push.

"It also says fresh pineapple can induce labor," he managed, his voice only slightly strained. "These are all unproven theories."

"Pineapple gives me heartburn," she said, making a face. "Not fun."

Ryan nodded and pulled her against him, needing the contact even as it tortured him. She fit perfectly under his arm, her head resting against his shoulder, her belly pressed against his side.

"I think we just need to relax," he said. "Watch a movie, keep your feet up. I've got soup cooking, and I made a salad. I'll heat up some rolls when you get hungry."

"I'm always hungry," she said, tilting her head to look up at him. Then her expression shifted, became more serious.

"You do realize that just as soon as the roads clear, I'm headed to Whitefish."

And there it was. The conversation he'd been trying to avoid.

"The doctor said as long as I went with you," he reminded her carefully. "Let's just wait and see what happens."

"I can drive myself." Her voice had that stubborn edge he was beginning to recognize.

Everything in him rebelled at the thought. "I don't think that's a good idea. If you broke down or the car went into a ditch, you'd be stranded. And that would probably be exactly when the baby decided to arrive." He took a breath, trying to find the right words. "I think you should stay here with me. Have the baby here in Missoula, and after that, we can decide what to do next."

Her hand found his, squeezing tight. "No. I want my mother with me."

The simple statement hit him harder than it should have. Of course, she wanted her mother. It was her first baby; she was scared, and she'd been alone through this whole pregnancy. He understood that. Respected it, even.

But it didn't make it easier to accept.

He reached out and cupped her face, his fingers threading through her soft hair. "I'm trying to keep you and the baby safe. I don't want anything bad to happen to you. I want our child to be born safe, here in Missoula, where I can take care of you both."

He could see the argument forming on her lips, could

see that stubborn determination in her eyes. So he did the only thing he could think of, he kissed her.

His mouth covered hers, swallowing whatever protest she'd been about to make. She melted into him immediately, her lips parting under his, her hand coming up to grip his shirt. The kiss was desperate, possessive, a claiming that had nothing to do with the argument they'd been having and everything to do with the need that had been building between them since the moment he'd recognized her in that hotel lobby.

His hands slipped beneath her sweater, running down the smooth, tight skin of her belly. And then—

A kick. Strong and definite against his palm.

"Oh." He broke the kiss, staring down at where his hand rested on her stomach. "Was that—?"

Amelia was smiling now, that soft, maternal smile that made his chest ache. She took his hand and moved it to a different spot. "She's been playing soccer all morning. Kicking me in the ribs, grabbing and tapping like she's saying 'let me out of here.'"

Ryan held perfectly still, waiting. And then it happened again, a distinct pressure against his palm, like their daughter was saying hello.

"That's incredible," he breathed. "That's our baby."

"That's our baby," Amelia confirmed.

Something inside him cracked open. He'd known, intellectually, that Amelia was pregnant with his child. But this, feeling his daughter move, feeling her alive and active inside her mother, made it real in a way nothing else had.

He slid down the loveseat until he was kneeling on the floor in front of Amelia. Slowly, giving her time to stop him if she wanted, he lifted her sweater to expose her swollen belly.

The sight of it, round and full and containing his child, made his throat tight.

"Hi, sweet girl," he said softly, hovering his lips above her skin. His hands spread across her stomach, and he felt Amelia shudder under his touch. "I can't wait to meet you. We're going to love you so very much. There are so many people who are going to be excited to see you, grandparents, uncles, and cousins."

His lips brushed her belly, pressing a gentle kiss there. "And your momma, she's going to be an amazing mother. The best mother. And I'm going to be your father. I'm going to protect you and love you and teach you everything I know." He smiled against her skin. "No boys until you're out of high school, by the way. That's non-negotiable."

Amelia leaned her head back and laughed, the sound rich and full. "No boys until she's out of high school? Like that's ever going to happen."

She pulled him up, and before he could process what was happening, her mouth was on his. This kiss was different from the last, deeper, more intentional. A promise, maybe. An acceptance of something neither of them had quite put into words yet.

When they broke apart, both breathing hard, Ryan

could see the desire in her eyes. The same desire was currently making it difficult for him to think straight.

"You're so beautiful, Amelia," he said, his voice rough. "I hope our daughter has your eyes, your nose, your perfect lips."

Unable to resist, he leaned down and kissed her stomach again. And then lower. And lower.

Her breathing became shallow, rapid. He could feel the tension in her body, the anticipation.

His fingers found the waistband of her sweatpants.

"Ryan." His name came out breathless. "Don't tease me. It's been nine long months."

The website had said it was safe. The doctor hadn't forbidden it. And God knew he wanted her with an intensity that bordered on painful.

But he wouldn't push. Wouldn't assume. This had to be her choice.

His lips continued their path down her stomach until he reached the elastic of her sweats. He looked up at her, making sure she was watching, making sure she understood what he was offering.

"Tell me to stop if this isn't what you want," he said. "I just want to make you happy."

A sigh escaped her, and she shifted on the loveseat, spreading her legs as much as her belly would allow. The invitation was clear.

Ryan's control snapped. He yanked her sweatpants down past her hips, past her thighs, exposing the soft skin he'd dreamed about for nine months. She was just as gorgeous as he remembered. More so, even, all curves and warmth and feminine perfection.

"Yes," she breathed. "Please. It's been so long."

He pressed a kiss to her inner thigh, then another higher up. "I've got you. Just relax and let me take care of you."

His hands slid up her legs, parting them further, and she made a sound, half moan, half whimper, that went straight through him.

"Ryan—"

"Shh. I've got you."

He kissed her again, higher this time, and she arched against him. Her hands found his hair, gripping tight, and he took that as all the encouragement he needed.

For nine months, he'd searched for her. For nine months, he'd wondered if he'd ever see her again, if he'd ever get the chance to touch her like this, to make her feel good, to show her without words how much she meant to him.

And now here she was, in his apartment, carrying his child, letting him worship her body the way he'd been desperate to do since the moment she'd walked away from him on that cruise ship.

He was not going to waste this second chance.

His mouth found her center, and she cried out, her hips bucking. He steadied her with his hands on her thighs, holding her in place as he worked her with his tongue, alternating between broad strokes and focused attention on the spot that made her gasp.

"Oh God," she moaned. "Ryan, I'm—I can't—"

"Let go," he murmured against her skin. "I've got you."

It didn't take long. She'd been wound tight, nine months of loneliness and fear and hormones coiling inside her, and now he was giving her permission to release it all. Her hands tightened in his hair, her thighs trembling against his shoulders, and then she was crying out his name as she came apart.

He worked her through it, gentling his touch as she became sensitive, pressing soft kisses to her inner thighs as she slowly came back down.

When he finally looked up, she was staring at him with wonder in her eyes, her cheeks flushed, her lips parted.

"That was..." She trailed off, seeming unable to find the words.

"Just the beginning," he promised, crawling back up her body to capture her mouth in a kiss. She could taste herself on his lips, and the way she moaned into his mouth made him hard enough to hurt.

"Your turn," she said when they broke apart, her hand sliding down his chest toward his waistband.

He caught her wrist, stopping her. "This was about you. About making you feel good."

"Ryan—"

"We have time," he said gently. "Right now, you need to rest. Keep your blood pressure down. Let me take care of you."

She looked like she wanted to argue, but another yawn caught her by surprise. The combination of pregnancy, travel, stress, and a powerful orgasm had clearly exhausted her.

"Fine," she grumbled, but she was smiling. "But you're not getting out of this. I owe you."

"I'll hold you to that," he said, pulling her sweats back up and adjusting her sweater. He grabbed her hand and pulled her up off the loveseat, pulling her towards the bedroom. He helped her into the bed and pulled the covers up around her.

"Now close your eyes for a bit. I'll wake you when the soup is ready."

"Stay with me?" Her voice was small, vulnerable.

"I'm not going anywhere," he promised, crawling in beside her and pulling her against his chest.

Within minutes, her breathing had evened out, her body relaxed against his. Ryan stared at the snow falling outside the window, at the white world that had trapped them together, and couldn't bring himself to regret a single moment of it.

She wanted to go to Whitefish. Wanted her family.

But maybe, just maybe, he could convince her that home could be here too. With him.

He had two weeks to make his case.

He intended to use every single day.

CHAPTER 12

When she awoke, Ryan was snuggled up against her in bed. His breathing was relaxed, and she knew he was asleep.

Amelia's heart hammered against her ribs. Nine months. Nine months since that incredible night on the cruise ship when Ryan had made her feel things she'd never felt before. Nine months of telling herself it had been a fantasy, a beautiful mistake, something that couldn't possibly be real.

Even though she was massive. Even though her belly was so swollen, she couldn't see her own feet. Even though everything about her body felt foreign and awkward and completely ungraceful.

Oh, how she wanted to feel him deep inside her once again. To see if the magic they had experienced that one night was still the same. She rubbed her buttocks against him.

"What are you doing?" he asked, his voice raw.

She couldn't face him, not yet. Especially if he said no.

"If you're not disgusted by my body, I'd like to try to have sex," she said, knowing it might be impossible.

"Honey, can't you feel how turned on I am?"

She sighed. "Yes, but…"

"Amelia, I want you today. I'll want you when you're old and gray. I'll even want you, when we're both so old that sex is just a distant memory."

She gave a little laugh. "And today?"

She rolled over and faced him.

"You're sure about this?" Ryan's voice was rough, strained. His eyes traced over her body with an intensity that made her skin flush hot.

"I've never been more sure of anything," she said, and meant it.

The truth was, she'd been sure of very little in her life lately. Sure, she'd always projected confidence, perfect Amelia Miller, the golden child, the one who had everything figured out. But beneath that carefully constructed facade, she'd been drowning in uncertainty since the moment that pregnancy test came back positive.

What kind of mother would she be? Could she handle raising a child alone? Would her family ever forgive her for the mess she'd made of things?

But this, being with Ryan, this felt right in a way nothing else had in months.

His hands found her hips, warm and steady, Amelia let out a breath she hadn't realized she'd been holding.

"Tell me if anything hurts," he murmured against the curve of her spine, pressing soft kisses along her shoulder blades. "Tell me if you need me to stop."

"I won't need you to stop," she whispered. "I need this. I need you."

The admission felt like peeling back armor she'd been wearing for years. Amelia Miller didn't need anyone. She was self-sufficient, independent, the sister who had it all together. Except she didn't. She never really had.

Ryan's hands moved over her body with careful attention, learning the new landscape of her curves. His touch was gentle but confident, and Amelia found herself relaxing into it, trusting him in a way that terrified her.

She'd spent her whole life being in control. Being the one who called the shots, who never let anyone see her weak or uncertain or vulnerable. But pregnancy had stripped away that illusion of control, left her raw and exposed and completely at the mercy of her own body.

And somehow, with Ryan, that didn't feel like weakness. It felt like freedom.

"You're so beautiful," he breathed against her ear, and she almost laughed.

Beautiful. Right. She was a beached whale, swollen and awkward and completely ungainly. But the way he looked at her, the way his hands worshipped every curve and swell of her changing body, made her almost believe him.

"I'm enormous," she said, trying to inject some humor into her voice even as emotion threatened to overwhelm her.

"You're carrying our child," Ryan said, and the possessiveness in his voice made something clench deep in her chest. "That makes you the most beautiful thing I've ever seen."

Our child. The words hung in the air between them, heavy with implication. This wasn't just about physical pleasure anymore, though God knew she wanted that desperately after nine months of celibacy. This was about something bigger, something that scared her more than labor ever could.

This was about whether they could be a family. Whether what they'd shared on that cruise ship had been real, or just a beautiful illusion that would shatter under the weight of reality.

Ryan positioned himself behind her, one hand steady on her hip, the other reaching around to caress her swollen belly. "Breathe," he murmured. "Just breathe and let me take care of you."

Let him take care of her. When was the last time Amelia had let anyone take care of her? She'd been the golden child, the achiever, the one who took care of everyone else. Even now, pregnant and scared and completely out of her depth, she'd been trying to handle everything alone.

But maybe that was the problem. Maybe she'd been alone for so long that she'd forgotten how to let someone in.

Ryan entered her slowly, carefully, from behind, giving her body time to adjust. The sensation was overwhelming, not just the physical pleasure, though that was intense enough to make her gasp, but the emotional intimacy of it. The vulnerability of letting him see her like this, of trusting him to be gentle with her when she was at her most fragile.

"Okay?" he asked, his voice strained with the effort of holding back.

"More than okay," she managed, her fingers clutching at the bedsheets. "Please, Ryan. Please move."

He set a slow, steady rhythm, each thrust careful and controlled. It was maddening and perfect all at once. Amelia wanted him to lose control, wanted him to take her with the same wild abandon they'd shared on the cruise ship. But she also appreciated his caution, his concern for her comfort, and the baby's safety.

The baby. Their baby. The tiny life they'd created together during one reckless, passionate night.

Tears pricked at Amelia's eyes, and she wasn't sure if it was from the physical pleasure building inside her or the emotional weight of the moment. Maybe both. Probably both.

"I missed you," she gasped as he moved inside her. "God, Ryan, I missed you so much."

"I'm here," he murmured, his hand sliding around to find the sensitive bundle of nerves that made her cry out. "I'm right here, and I'm not going anywhere."

Not going anywhere. Could she believe that? Could she trust that this wasn't just about the baby, that he actually wanted her for more than just obligation and responsibility?

Amelia had spent her whole life being wanted for what

she could do, what she could achieve, how she could make other people look good. Her parents loved her accomplishments. Men dated her because she looked good on their arm, because she was successful and polished and the kind of woman you introduced to your colleagues.

But Ryan had wanted her before he knew about the baby. He'd chosen her that night on the cruise ship when she'd been nobody special, just another passenger looking for an escape from reality.

The thought made something crack open inside her chest, and suddenly she was crying in earnest, tears streaming down her face even as pleasure built inside her body.

"Amelia?" Ryan's voice was concerned, his movements slowing. "Are you okay? Do you need me to stop?"

"Don't stop," she sobbed. "Please don't stop. I—I need—"

She couldn't articulate what she needed. Maybe she didn't even know herself. But Ryan seemed to understand anyway, his arms wrapping around her as much as her belly would allow, holding her steady while she fell apart.

"I've got you," he whispered against her shoulder. "Let go, Amelia. I've got you."

And she did. She let go of the control she'd been clinging to for so long, let herself feel everything she'd been holding back for nine months. The fear and the loneliness and the desperate hope that maybe, just maybe, she didn't have to do this alone.

The orgasm built slowly, pleasure coiling tighter and tighter in her core. Ryan's fingers worked their magic while he moved inside her, and Amelia felt herself spiraling higher and higher, chasing something just out of reach.

"That's it," Ryan encouraged, his voice rough with his own need. "Let me feel you come apart."

Come apart. That's exactly what she was doing, coming apart at the seams, all her carefully constructed defenses crumbling under the weight of her feelings for this man.

She loved him. The realization hit her at the same moment the orgasm did, stealing her breath and making stars burst behind her eyelids. She loved Ryan with a ferocity that terrified her, loved him in a way she'd never loved anyone before.

"Ryan!" His name tore from her throat as pleasure crashed through her in waves, her body clenching around him as she shattered.

He followed her over the edge moments later, his own release shuddering through him as he held her tight. They stayed like that for a long moment, both of them trembling and gasping for breath, neither willing to break the connection.

Finally, carefully, Ryan eased out of her and helped her roll onto her back. He curled around her, one arm draped protectively over her belly, and Amelia felt something settle inside her chest.

This. This was what she'd been missing her whole life. Not just the physical pleasure, though that had been incredible, but this feeling of being truly seen and cherished and loved.

"That was..." Ryan trailed off, apparently unable to find the words.

"Yeah," Amelia agreed, her voice thick with emotion. "It really was."

They lay in comfortable silence for a while, Ryan's hand gently stroking her belly. Amelia felt the baby move, a strong kick against her ribs, and she smiled despite the tears still drying on her cheeks.

"I love you," she said suddenly, the words spilling out before she could stop them. "I know it's too soon, and I know we barely know each other, and I know I'm probably just emotional because I'm pregnant and we just had sex, but—"

"Amelia." Ryan's voice was gentle but firm, cutting off her rambling. "Breathe."

She took a shaky breath, waiting for him to let her down easy. To tell her she was right, it was too soon, they needed to take things slow for the baby's sake.

"I love you too," he said instead, and Amelia's heart stuttered in her chest. "I've been in love with you since that night on the cruise ship. Maybe even before that, from the moment I saw you at the bar looking lost and lonely and so damn beautiful I could barely breathe."

"Really?" The word came out small, uncertain. So unlike her usual confident self.

"Really," Ryan confirmed, pressing a kiss to her shoulder. "I know we have a lot to figure out. I know this is complicated and messy and nothing like either of us probably imagined. But I want this, Amelia. I want you, and I want our baby, and I want to build a life together if you'll let me."

More tears spilled down her cheeks, but these were different. These were happy tears, relieved tears, tears of someone who'd been carrying a burden alone for so long and finally realized she didn't have to anymore.

"I want that too," she whispered. "I'm terrified, but I want it."

"Good," Ryan said, and she could hear the smile in his voice. "Because I'm not going anywhere. You're stuck with me now."

Stuck with him. Amelia turned that thought over in her mind, expecting to feel trapped or suffocated the way she usually did when men got too serious. But instead, she just felt... safe. Cherished. Home.

"My family is going to have a field day with this," she said, trying to inject some levity into the moment. "Perfect Amelia, knocked up by a guy she met on a cruise, showing up for Christmas with a baby daddy in tow."

"Is that what I am?" Ryan asked, amusement coloring his tone. "Your baby daddy?"

"What would you prefer? Significant other? Partner? Man who knocked me up and is now contractually obligated to stick around?"

Ryan laughed, the sound rumbling through his chest and into her back. "How about fiancé?"

Amelia's breath caught. "What?"

"Marry me," Ryan said, and it wasn't a question. "Not because of the baby, though I'm grateful for her. Not because it's the right thing to do or what people expect. Marry me because I love you and I want to spend the rest of my life making you happy."

"That's the worst proposal ever," Amelia said, but she was laughing through her tears. "You're supposed to get down on one knee and have a ring and—"

"I don't have a ring yet," Ryan admitted. "But I'll get you whatever you want. Something big and sparkly that tells everyone you're mine."

"I don't need big and sparkly," Amelia said, surprising herself. The old Amelia would have demanded the biggest diamond, the most impressive display. But now? Now she just wanted him. "I just need you."

"Is that a yes?"

Amelia turned as much as her belly would allow, meeting Ryan's eyes in the dim light of the bedroom. She saw love there, and determination, and a promise of forever.

"Yes," she whispered. "It's a yes."

He kissed her then, slow and deep and full of promise. And for the first time in nine months, maybe for the first time in her life, Amelia Miller felt like she was exactly where she was supposed to be.

The baby kicked again, as if in approval, and they both laughed.

"I think she approves," Ryan said, his hand finding the spot where their daughter was moving.

"She better," Amelia said. "Since this is all her fault anyway."

"Best mistake I ever made," Ryan murmured, pulling her close again.

And lying there in his arms, feeling their baby move between them and knowing that this messy, complicated, unexpected life was really hers, Amelia had to agree.

Best mistake ever.

CHAPTER 13

Ryan was nervous. Yes, he wanted to be with Amelia, but he didn't want to harm her or their baby. He wanted that little baby girl to stay inside Amelia until it was time for her to come out.

Already, he loved that child and was well on the way to falling for Amelia.

Ryan lay in the darkness, listening to Amelia's breathing even out beside him. She'd finally fallen asleep, one hand resting protectively on her belly, the other curled beneath her cheek like a child. Even in sleep, she looked exhausted, dark circles under her eyes, her face still slightly puffy from the tears she'd shed.

But lying here now, with the woman he loved carrying his child, Ryan felt the full weight of what they'd just done. Not the sex, though that had been incredible, even better than he remembered from the cruise ship. No, what overwhelmed him was the confession. The promises they'd made to each other.

Ryan turned his head to study Amelia's face in the dim light filtering through the curtains. Even exhausted and pregnant and vulnerable in ways she'd probably hate if she knew he was watching, she was the most beautiful woman he'd ever seen.

He'd meant every word he'd said. He loved her. He wanted to marry her. He wanted to build a life with her and their daughter, wanted to wake up next to her every morning for the rest of his life.

The certainty of it should have terrified him. Ryan had always been careful, calculated, the kind of guy who made pro-and-con lists before making major decisions.

But with Amelia? There were no calculations, no careful considerations. Just this bone-deep knowledge that she was his, that their baby was his, that this messy, complicated situation was exactly where he was supposed to be.

The baby kicked against his palm where it rested on Amelia's belly, and Ryan's throat tightened. His daughter. In a matter of weeks, maybe days, given how low Amelia was carrying, he was going to be a father for the second time in his life.

The thought sent both terror and exhilaration through him, but the terror won out because he'd failed once before. Failed when it mattered most.

Sandy. Charlotte.

Their names echoed through his mind like a prayer he'd

never stopped saying. His wife. His daughter. Gone for three years now, but the guilt was as fresh as the day he'd lost them.

He needed to tell Amelia. She deserved to know why he was so protective, why the thought of her traveling in a blizzard made his chest constrict with panic. Why he kept checking the weather reports obsessively, why every gust of wind against the windows made his pulse spike.

But how did you tell the woman you loved that you'd already lost a family? That weather, cruel, indifferent weather, had stolen everything from him once before?

Could he be a better husband this time? A better father? Could he keep them safe when he'd failed so spectacularly before?

He had to be. Failure wasn't an option. Not again.

Amelia shifted in her sleep, a small sound of discomfort escaping her lips. Ryan immediately moved closer, adjusting the pillow beneath her belly, making sure she was comfortable. She settled again with a soft sigh, and something in his chest cracked open.

This. This was what love felt like. Not the heart-pounding excitement of new attraction, though he felt that too. But this deeper thing, this desperate need to take care of her, to make sure she never hurt or felt alone or scared again.

He'd felt it before, with Sandy. That fierce, protective love that made you willing to do anything, sacrifice anything, to keep your family safe.

And he'd failed.

Ryan closed his eyes against the memory, but it came anyway. It always did in quiet moments like this. His ambulance responding to the call. The drive through the snowstorm, too late, always too late. Sandy's car rolled in the ditch. Charlotte's car seat empty because she'd been thrown from the vehicle.

His wife and four-year-old daughter, gone in an instant because he'd let them drive in dangerous weather. Because he'd been at work, he couldn't leave his shift, and had told Sandy to just be careful and everything would be fine.

Everything will be fine.

Famous last words.

He thought back to that night on the cruise ship, trying to understand why he'd let himself fall so completely for Amelia. Was it when he'd first spotted her at the bar, laughing with her friend, and lovely in that blue dress? He'd been on that cruise to escape the memories, to try to move forward after three years of being stuck in grief.

Maybe it had been when she'd kissed him first, bold and brave and so different from the carefully controlled woman she presented to the world. For the first time since Sandy died, he'd felt alive again. Like maybe he deserved a second chance at happiness.

Or in the morning, when she'd slipped out of his room without saying goodbye and he'd felt like someone had carved out a piece of his chest all over again.

She'd vanished like Cinderella, leaving him with nothing but memories and a longing he couldn't shake. And the fear that maybe he didn't deserve a second chance after all. That maybe losing her was the universe's way of reminding him that people he loved didn't stick around.

And now she was here, in his arms, carrying his baby. Life had a funny way of working out.

Or a cruel way of offering him everything he wanted just so it could take it away again.

Amelia's phone buzzed on the nightstand, the screen lighting up with a text notification. Ryan glanced at it automatically, not meaning to pry, but the name made him freeze.

Mom: Where are you? Please tell me you're okay.

Ryan felt something twist in his gut. Amelia had mentioned her sisters, Emma, the invisible one, and Olivia, the misfit. And Amelia herself, the golden child who always had to be perfect, who could never let anyone see her struggle.

She was going to walk into that house, nine months pregnant and engaged to a man her family had never met. A man who'd gotten her pregnant on a one-night stand during a cruise ship fling.

The golden child's fall from grace would be spectacular.

Ryan's jaw tightened. He didn't give a damn what her family thought. He loved Amelia and was going to marry her. Anyone who made her feel bad about it would have to go through him first.

But he knew it mattered to her. For all her bravado and confidence, Amelia cared desperately what her family thought. She'd spent her whole life trying to be perfect for them, trying to earn their approval and admiration.

How would they react when they saw her? Would they judge her? Shame her? Make her feel like she'd disappointed them?

Ryan's hand curled protectively over her belly. Over their daughter. Over his second chance at being a father.

He wouldn't let anyone hurt her. Not her family, not judgmental strangers, not anyone. Amelia was his now, and he protected what was his.

This time, he wouldn't fail.

The fierceness of the feeling surprised him. Ryan had never been a particularly aggressive guy. He was a paramedic; his job was to save lives, to help people, and to stay calm in crisis situations. He prided himself on his level head and steady hands.

But after losing Sandy and Charlotte, something had changed in him. He'd become more protective, more cautious. Maybe too cautious. His friends had told him he needed therapy, needed to work through his survivor's guilt.

But the thought of anyone making Amelia feel less than perfect, less than cherished, less than absolutely worthy of love? That made him want to put his fist through a wall.

Easy, he told himself. *She doesn't need you to fight her battles. She needs you to stand beside her while she fights them herself.*

That was the thing about Amelia, she was strong. Stronger than she gave herself credit for. She'd been handling this pregnancy alone for nine months, working as a lawyer, never complaining or asking for help, even though she must have been terrified.

She didn't need him to rescue her. She needed him to be her partner. Her equal. Someone who loved her not in spite of her mess but because of it, because her imperfections made her real and human and so much more than the perfect facade she showed the world.

Just like Sandy had been.

God, he missed Sandy. Missed her laugh, her terrible cooking, the way she'd always known exactly what to say when he'd had a bad day at work. But he'd learned something in the three years since her death: you could love someone who was gone and still open your heart to someone new. The love didn't replace or diminish, it just grew to make room for more.

Sandy would have liked Amelia, he thought. Would have told him to stop overthinking and just be happy.

But happiness felt dangerous when you'd already lost everything once.

Amelia stirred again, her eyes fluttering open. For a moment, she looked disoriented, confused about where she was. Then her gaze found his, and she smiled, soft and vulnerable and completely unguarded.

"Hi," she whispered.

"Hi yourself," Ryan said, brushing a strand of hair from her face. "How are you feeling?"

"Sore," she admitted. "And happy. And terrified. All at the same time."

"Me too," Ryan confessed. "Except for the sore part."

Amelia laughed, the sound light and genuine. Then her expression grew serious. "Did you mean it? What you said before?"

"Every word," Ryan said without hesitation. "I love you, Amelia. I want to marry you. I want to be there when our daughter is born, and for her first steps, and her first day of school, and every moment in between. I want to build a life with you."

I want to do it right this time.

"Even though we barely know each other?"

"We know the important things," Ryan said. "I know you're brave and beautiful and stronger than you think. I know you cry at sad commercials and you hate the taste of coffee but drink it anyway because you think it makes you look professional. I know you love your family even though they make you crazy, and you're terrified of being a bad mother even though you're going to be amazing at it."

Amelia's eyes filled with tears. "How do you know all that?"

"Because I pay attention," Ryan said simply. "Because when you love someone, you notice things. And I've been paying attention to you since the moment we met."

She was quiet for a long moment, her fingers tracing patterns on his chest. Over the place where his heart had been shattered and was slowly learning to beat again.

"I'm scared," she finally admitted. "What if we're making a mistake? What if this is just hormones and proximity and we wake up in six months and realize we can't stand each other?"

"Then we'll figure it out," Ryan said, though the words felt hollow. He'd thought he and Sandy would have forever to figure things out. Life had taught him that forever was a luxury, not a guarantee. "Together. That's what marriage is, right? Figuring out how to make it work even when it's hard."

"You make it sound so simple."

"Maybe it is," Ryan said. "Maybe we're the ones making it complicated."

Amelia smiled, but it didn't quite reach her eyes. "My family is going to lose their minds. I'm going to show up pregnant with a guy they've never heard of and announce we're getting married."

"So we'll tell them the truth," Ryan said. "That we met, we fell in love, and we're having a baby. In that order, even if the timeline is a little compressed."

"You think they'll understand?"

"I think it doesn't matter if they do or don't," Ryan said gently. "This is our life, Amelia. Our choice. We don't need their permission or their approval. We just need each other."

She looked up at him, and Ryan saw the exact moment she let go of whatever fear she'd been holding onto. Saw her decide to trust him, to trust this, to take the leap.

But then something shifted in her expression. Her hand moved to her belly, and her eyes went distant.

"I know you think we should wait, but I can't." Tears started streaming down her face again, and Ryan didn't think these were happy tears. "My mother's text. What if something's wrong? What if that's why she wanted us all home for Christmas?"

"Hey, shhh, it's going to be all right," Ryan said, pulling her close despite the panic clawing at his throat. The thought of her out on those roads, in this weather... "You can stay here as long as you need. You could have the baby here in Missoula. There's a good hospital—"

"No," she said firmly, pulling back to look at him. "If it stops snowing, I'm going on to Whitefish. I want my mother there when I have this child. I want my family."

"What about me?" The words came out sharper than he'd intended, laced with old hurt and new fear.

"Of course you," she said, her hand finding his face. "But only if you come to Whitefish with me."

Ryan closed his eyes, his jaw clenching so hard it ached. "I'm just worried the weather isn't going to let us get to Whitefish safely. You and the baby's safety are my top priority."

Because I already lost a family to weather. Because I can't lose you too.

"I fear us getting stuck on the highway with you going into labor. No hospital nearby, no help coming, just—" His voice broke, and he had to stop.

Amelia's eyes widened, and he realized she'd heard something in his voice. Some echo of old pain he hadn't meant to let slip.

"Ryan?" Her voice was soft, concerned.

"I just need you safe," he finally managed. "Both of you. Safe is all that matters."

Amelia studied his face for a long moment, and he knew she could tell there was more to the story. But she didn't push. Instead, she started to cry again, deep, shuddering sobs that shook her whole body.

"I understand," she gasped between tears. "But I want to go home. Call it pregnancy jitters, whatever you want, but I need to be in Whitefish. My mother asked us all to come home for Christmas, and I'm so afraid something is wrong. Unless this baby comes right now, I'm going."

Ryan felt his world tilting. He couldn't stop her. If she decided to leave, all he could do was go with her or watch her drive away.

And watching another woman he loved drive away into dangerous weather? That wasn't going to happen.

Never again.

"Okay," he said, the word tasting like defeat and terror and love all mixed together. "Okay. But we wait until the roads are clear. We check the weather every hour. And at the first sign of trouble, we turn around. Deal?"

"Deal," Amelia whispered, pressing her face against his chest.

Ryan held her close, listening to the wind howl outside, feeling his daughter kick against his palm. Soon, he needed to tell Amelia about Sandy and Charlotte. Soon, she needed to understand why he felt this way, why the thought of losing her made him feel like he was drowning.

But tonight, he just held her and prayed that this time, *please, God, this time,* he could keep the people he loved safe.

This time, he wouldn't fail.

CHAPTER 14

The next morning, Amelia woke to the now-familiar sound of wind howling against the windows and the soft patter of snow hitting glass. She didn't even need to look outside to know the storm was still raging. Three days now. Three days of being trapped in Ryan's apartment while the blizzard raged outside.

Her bladder dragged her from the warmth of the bed, again. This was the fourth time tonight, and each trip to the bathroom felt like climbing Mount Everest. Everything was harder when you were carrying an extra forty pounds and had a tiny human using your bladder as a trampoline.

She shuffled to the bathroom in the dark, not wanting to wake Ryan, and took care of business. When she caught sight of herself in the mirror, she barely recognized the woman staring back. Dark circles under her eyes. Hair tangled and wild. Her face fuller than it had been nine months ago.

This was not how she'd pictured having her first child.

She'd dreamed about it, of course. What woman didn't? In her fantasy, there had been a wedding first, something elegant but not ostentatious, maybe in a garden with her family surrounding her. Then she and her husband would have planned the pregnancy, would have watched her belly grow together, gone to doctor's appointments holding hands, picked out nursery colors, and argued over baby names.

Instead, she'd been alone for nine months. No wedding. No husband. Just her and a baby she'd accidentally created with a man whose last name she hadn't even known.

When she crawled back into bed, Ryan stirred slightly but didn't wake. She lay there in the darkness, listening to his steady breathing, studying his profile in the dim light filtering through the curtains.

Now she'd found him. Against all odds, in the middle of a blizzard, she'd found the father of her baby.

And as much as she adored him, and she realized she loved him, she was terrified.

Terrified he wasn't the right man. Terrified, this feeling between them was just proximity and circumstance rather than something real. Terrified he'd wake up one morning and realize that being saddled with an instant family wasn't what he wanted after all. Terrified he'd walk away, and she'd have to watch her daughter grow up wondering why her father didn't love her enough to stay.

Terrified he'd break her heart a second time, and this time she wouldn't recover.

But he wasn't running. That was the thing that kept surprising her. He'd embraced her and this baby whole-heartedly, without hesitation, without conditions. He talked about being there for the birth as if it were a privilege rather than an obligation. He'd welcomed her into his home, cooked for her, taken care of her, kissed her belly, and whispered to their daughter through her skin.

Staring at him in the semi-darkness, Amelia felt something shift in her chest. Something dangerous and wonderful and absolutely terrifying.

On the ship, she'd been attracted to him, powerfully, overwhelmingly attracted. But she'd told herself it was just physical, just vacation chemistry enhanced by tropical drinks and the freedom of being away from real life. When the cruise ended and she realized she'd made a huge mistake not leaving her number, she tried to convince herself she was just hung up on great sex.

Then she'd learned she was pregnant, and finding him had become urgent for entirely different reasons.

But now, lying in his bed, watching him sleep, feeling safe for the first time in months, now she was beginning to understand that what she felt went deeper than attraction or circumstance or even their baby.

Damn, the man was beautiful. On the ship, he'd been tanned and sun-bronzed, all easy smiles and relaxed vacation energy. Now, in the grey morning light, he looked different, scruffier, more real, somehow even more attractive. She could see the shadow of stubble on his jaw, the way his dark lashes rested against his cheeks, the small scar above his right eyebrow that she'd never noticed before.

She hoped their baby had some of his features. Those emerald eyes. That strong jaw. That smile that made her forget to breathe.

Throughout high school, college, even law school, she'd dated. She'd been the head cheerleader who could have had anyone she wanted, and she'd enjoyed the attention. But she'd never found someone who made her want forever. Never felt that bone-deep certainty that said *this one, this is the one.*

She'd lost her virginity in college to a boyfriend she'd dated for six months and felt nothing beyond pleasant physical satisfaction. There had been one other man after that, a fellow law student who'd been brilliant and ambitious and utterly wrong for her. And then Ryan, nine months ago, who'd made her feel things she didn't know were possible.

Why did this man make her want to settle down? Make her think about marriage and family and building a life together? Was it just because she was pregnant, her hormones convincing her that the father of her baby was her soulmate?

No. She'd felt this way that night on the cruise, before she'd known about the baby, before there were any stakes beyond a vacation fling.

Amelia sighed and tried to roll to her side, but nothing was comfortable anymore. Her hips ached. Her back throbbed. The baby seemed to be using her ribcage as a jungle gym. No matter how she positioned herself, some part of her body protested.

She was so tired of being pregnant. Tired of carrying all this extra weight. Tired of not being able to see her feet or bend over or sleep through the night.

Two more weeks. Just two more weeks, and she'd meet her daughter. Two more weeks, and she'd know if labor was as terrifying as she feared. Two more weeks, and everything would change.

She gazed at Ryan again, memorizing the planes of his face. She wanted to know everything about him. His favorite foods. His views on politics and religion and whether he believed in ghosts. His first memory. His biggest fear. What made him laugh, what made him cry, what his family was like beyond the basics he'd told her.

She didn't want to lose him again.

Suddenly, the baby kicked her, hard, right up under her ribs in that spot that made it impossible to breathe. Amelia gasped, her hand flying to her side.

Ryan jerked awake immediately, his eyes flying open, his hand reaching for her. "What's wrong? Are you in labor?"

The concern on his face, the immediate alertness, the way his hand instinctively went to her belly, it all made warmth spread through her chest.

"Sorry," she said, catching her breath. "The baby kicked me in the ribs. She's really active this morning."

Relief flooded his expression, followed by a smile that transformed his whole face. His hand moved across her belly, gentle and reverent. "I can tell she's going to be a little troublemaker. Is she going to be as stubborn as her mother?"

Amelia felt herself smile despite the lingering ache in her ribs. "I hope so. Stubbornness has gotten me far in life."

"I've noticed," he said dryly, but his eyes were warm with affection. He snuggled closer, wrapping himself around her and their baby as much as her belly would allow. "I hope she has your blonde hair and your intelligence."

"You think I'm smart?" The question came out more vulnerable than she'd intended.

"Oh yes." His voice was certain, matter-of-fact. "I watched you all week on that cruise. You sized people up within minutes, made judgments about who was genuine and who was putting on a show. It was impressive."

"That's what makes me a good lawyer," she said. "I like to figure out why people do the things they do. What motivates them. What they're hiding."

"Have you thought about starting your own practice?" Ryan asked. "Especially now that you're not tied to Cheyenne anymore?"

Amelia had thought about it. Thought about it long and hard during the endless days of unemployment. "I want more experience first. Not just preparing wills and handling incorporations. For me, the excitement is in the courtroom, proving my client's innocence or proving they've been wronged. Eventually, I might go out on my own. But right now, I want to work for someone who can teach me."

Being fired had been devastating. She was the golden child, the one who'd never failed at anything. Being let go felt like flunking a test she'd studied for her entire life.

"Why didn't you sue them?" Ryan's voice was quiet but intense. "The firm that fired you. That was discrimination."

Amelia gave a bitter laugh. "Because to get my severance package, which I desperately needed, I had to sign an agreement that I wouldn't sue for discrimination. I was about five months along when they realized I wasn't just gaining weight. I was an embarrassment to them. A stain on their respectable image."

The meeting with HR still made her stomach turn. The way they'd couched everything in corporate language, talking about "fit" and "direction" and "mutual benefit." The severance agreement they'd slid across the table, already prepared, already anticipating her signature.

She'd needed that money. Needed the insurance extension to cover the birth. So she'd signed, even though every instinct had screamed at her to fight.

"They're asshats," Ryan said flatly.

"Yes, they are," Amelia agreed. "But someday, karma will catch up with them. Maybe I'll face them in court on opposite sides of a case. That's the dream that gets me through."

Just then, the baby kicked again, and Ryan's face lit up. "I think she agrees with you."

His hand stayed on her belly, feeling their daughter

move, and Amelia felt that dangerous warmth spread through her chest again.

"I love having you here in my bed," Ryan said softly, his eyes meeting hers.

The words hung between them, heavy with implication. Not just *I love having you here,* but specifically *in my bed.* Together. Intimate. Like this was where she belonged.

"I like being here," she admitted, her voice barely above a whisper.

Ryan smiled, then suddenly pushed himself upright with an energy she didn't feel. "Come on. We have a busy day ahead of us."

Amelia blinked at him. "Last I checked, it was still snowing."

"It is," he confirmed, already climbing out of bed. "But some of the town streets have been cleared. I called my mom last night after you fell asleep. I want you to meet my family."

Fear shot through her, sharp and immediate. "But I'm nine months pregnant with your child. We're not married. We barely know each other."

"And they're going to be thrilled for us," Ryan said with absolute confidence. "My mother knew I met someone on the cruise, I talked about you nonstop for months. I'll tell her we found each other again."

Amelia sat up slowly, her mind racing. After her experience with the law firm, she'd more or less hidden away in her apartment. Unmarried and pregnant felt like wearing a scarlet letter. She'd convinced herself she didn't care what people thought, but the truth was, every judgmental look had cut deeper than she wanted to admit.

"If they judge me—" she started.

"They won't," Ryan interrupted firmly. "My family isn't like that. And even if anyone did say something, which they won't, I'd shut it down immediately. No one disrespects you or our baby. Not while I'm around."

The fierceness in his voice made her chest tight.

"If you're certain," she said slowly.

"I'm certain." He was already pulling clothes from his dresser. "They're going to be excited for us. My mother's been waiting for grandchildren for years. Now get ready, she's expecting us for lunch."

Nerves fluttered in Amelia's stomach. This was Ryan's family she was about to meet. His parents. His brothers. People who would be part of her daughter's life regardless of what happened between her and Ryan.

She wanted to make a good impression. Needed to make a good impression.

But more than that, she realized, she wanted them to like her. Wanted them to accept her. Wanted to feel like maybe, just maybe, she could belong here.

Even if Whitefish was still calling her home.

CHAPTER 15

Ryan had called his mother the night before, after Amelia had fallen asleep with her head on his shoulder. The conversation had been brief, whispered so he wouldn't wake her, but critically important.

"Don't mention Sandy and Charlotte," he'd said. "Please, Mom. Not a word. I haven't told her yet."

There had been a long pause on the other end of the line. Then his mother's quiet voice: "When are you going to tell her, sweetheart?"

"Tonight. After we leave. When we're alone."

"She needs to know, Ryan."

"I know. And she will. I just... I want one day where there are no comparisons. One day where this is just about Amelia. A fresh start."

His mother had agreed, though he could hear the concern in her voice. She'd make sure his father and brothers knew too. No one would say anything.

Because Ryan needed this to be separate. His old life and his new life couldn't be tangled together, not yet. He'd loved Sandy and Charlotte more than anything in the world, would always love them, but they were gone. It had taken him two years to crawl out of the darkness their deaths had left behind.

Somehow, he'd kept from telling his mother she was pregnant. About how they were expecting a baby. But soon she would know, and he knew they would be thrilled.

Now, with Amelia, he had a chance at happiness again. At a family. At a future.

Watching her over the past three days, seeing her navigate her fears, feeling their baby kick under his palm, listening to her talk about her dreams and her family, it had all cemented what he'd suspected since that night on the cruise.

This woman was it for him.

Call him old-fashioned, but this child deserved to have his last name. Deserved to have parents who were committed to each other, not just co-parenting from separate cities.

He'd spent the morning preparing. Shoveled the walkway from his apartment to the parking lot, clearing every inch of snow and ice. Started the Jeep early so it would be warm. Made sure Amelia was bundled up in her coat, scarf, and gloves before they even stepped outside.

Now, as he gripped her arm and guided her carefully across the cleared pavement, his heart hammered with nervous anticipation.

"No slip and falls," he said, his voice coming out more tense than he'd intended. "Our little accident needs a couple more weeks in the oven."

Amelia held onto him tightly, her fingers digging into his coat sleeve. "If I start falling, you know I'll take you down with me."

"Not going to happen," he said firmly. If she started to fall, he'd make damn sure she landed on top of him, that his body cushioned hers and protected their baby. But that wasn't going to be necessary. He wouldn't let her fall.

"But you're not going to fall," he added, guiding her to the passenger side and opening the door.

He lifted her, God, she was getting heavy, though he'd never tell her that, and settled her onto the seat. She looked up at him with a mixture of gratitude and exasperation.

"Jeeps are not made for pregnant women," she said.

"No," he agreed with a grin, "but they do great in the snow. It's how I get to work when everyone else is stuck at home."

He closed her door and jogged around to the driver's side, his breath forming clouds in the frigid air. The temperature had to be in the single digits, and with the wind chill, it felt even colder.

The roads were a slick mess as they pulled out of the apartment complex. Even though the city had plowed and salted, there were still patches of ice, still dangerous spots where the Jeep's tires struggled for traction.

"This is why I don't want you driving to Whitefish," he

said, gripping the steering wheel tighter as they navigated a turn.

Amelia sighed beside him. "I know."

"These roads are plowed, and they're still dangerous. The highway, I can guarantee you, hasn't been touched. Until it reopens, the plows won't go out there. Until the storm stops and the sun comes out, they'll leave it alone."

"The weatherman said it's supposed to stop snowing tomorrow," Amelia said quietly.

A blast of wind slammed into the Jeep, pushing it toward the center line. Ryan fought the steering wheel, his jaw clenched, every muscle tensed. When he finally had control again, he exhaled slowly.

"We'll see," he said.

He knew he'd end up driving her to Whitefish. Knew it in his bones. She wanted to be with her family for Christmas, wanted her mother at the birth, and he wasn't going to deny her that. But God, he didn't want to make that drive. Didn't want to risk her and their baby on icy highways in the middle of winter.

It was part of why he'd insisted on this visit today, to explain to his mother why he wouldn't be there for Christmas. Why he'd be in Whitefish instead, with Amelia's family, making sure she and the baby were safe.

And maybe, just maybe, his mother could help convince Amelia to stay in Missoula instead.

The death of Sandy and Charlotte had devastated his entire family. His mother had barely functioned for months. His father had aged ten years overnight. His brothers had rallied around him, taking turns staying at his house, making sure he ate, making sure he didn't do anything stupid in his grief.

Today, they would be shocked. But they'd also be happy, so incredibly happy, to learn he was expecting another child.

It would be a complete surprise. Unless his brother Clint had heard something at the hospital, which was possible. Hospital gossip spread faster than wildfire.

Ryan was so lost in thought that he almost didn't see the car sliding through the red light ahead. Almost didn't react in time.

He slammed on the brakes, his hand shooting out instinctively to brace Amelia as the Jeep skidded to a stop. The other car missed them by inches, maybe a foot at most, sliding sideways through the intersection before straightening out and continuing down the road like nothing had happened.

"Oh crap," Amelia gasped, her hand pressed to her chest. "That was scary."

"And my reasoning for not wanting to drive far," Ryan said through gritted teeth. His heart was racing, adrenaline flooding his system. That had been close. Too close.

He could have lost them both. Right there. In an instant.

"I'd be safe with you," Amelia said softly. "If you drove me in this beast of a vehicle, we could make it to Whitefish."

He kept his eyes on the road, navigating the slick streets with renewed caution. "We'll talk about it tonight."

Tonight, after he told her about Sandy and Charlotte. After she understood why he was so terrified of icy highways. After she knew that he'd already lost a wife and child to a winter accident, and the thought of losing her and their baby the same way made him physically ill.

Sandy had been an excellent driver in snow. Cautious. Careful. It hadn't mattered. The semi-truck that hit them had lost control on black ice, and there was nothing she could have done to avoid it.

The insurance settlement had been substantial. Enough that Ryan could have stopped working, could have taken years off to grieve. But he'd rather have his wife and daughter. Would give every penny back if it meant holding them one more time.

He pulled up to his parents' house, a ranch-style home in a quiet neighborhood where he'd grown up. Michael's car was in the driveway, his youngest brother had flown in from college before the storm hit. Tyler's truck was there too.

His father had left him a spot under the carport that connected to the garage, sheltered from the worst of the weather. But even there, melting snow had created a treacherous sheet of ice.

"You wait right there," Ryan said, putting the Jeep in park. "I'll come around and help you."

"Don't worry," Amelia said with a wry smile. "I don't think I could crawl out of here without your help anyway."

Ryan climbed out, the cold air hitting him like a slap. He said a silent prayer as he walked around to the passenger side. Please let them love her. Please let this go well.

When he opened her door, Amelia was already shifting forward, trying to figure out the best way to dismount from the high seat. He reached up and gripped her waist, steadying her.

Her foot slipped on the running board, ice and snow had accumulated despite his best efforts, and she gasped, her hands flying to his shoulders. But he had her. He wasn't going to let her fall.

"That was close," he said once she was safely on the ground, his hands still on her waist.

"Yes," she breathed, her eyes wide. "Thank you."

"Anytime."

He took her arm and guided her carefully through the garage and into the house. His heart was pounding again, but this time it wasn't from fear of falling. This time it was anticipation.

"Hello," he called out as they stepped into the mudroom.

He heard movement from the kitchen, and then his mother appeared in the doorway. Her eyes went immediately to Amelia, and her mouth fell open.

Ryan watched his mother take in every detail, Amelia's obvious pregnancy, the way she held Ryan's arm, the nervousness in her expression.

"Son," his mother said, walking toward them slowly.

"Mom, I'd like you to meet Amelia." Ryan's voice was steady, proud. "She's the girl I met on the cruise."

His mother's gaze moved between them, understanding dawning in her eyes.

"Nice to meet you," she said, recovering quickly though Ryan could see the shock still lingering.

"And yes," Ryan added, unable to keep the grin off his face, "that's my baby she's carrying."

For a moment, everything was still. Silent.

Then his mother's eyes filled with tears, happy tears, and she rushed forward, pulling Amelia into a hug that was both gentle and fierce.

"Thank God," his mother whispered. "Finally. He found you."

"Yes," Amelia said, smiling over his mother's shoulder at Ryan. "We both searched for each other."

His mother pulled back, wiping her eyes, and called out: "Brent! Boys! Get in here and meet Amelia!"

Within seconds, the house erupted with noise. His father emerged from his study, reading glasses still perched on his nose. Clint came down the stairs, Michael and Tyler right behind him. They all crowded into the entryway, staring at Amelia with various degrees of shock and curiosity.

"This is Amelia," his mother said, her arm still around Amelia's shoulders. "And she's going to have Ryan's baby."

His brothers moved first, all three of them coming forward to hug Amelia gently, then turning to slap Ryan on the back and mutter congratulations. Clint's hug lasted a little longer, and when he pulled back, his eyes were suspiciously bright.

"About time," Clint whispered. "You deserve this."

Ryan's father was the last to approach. He walked slowly, his eyes taking in every detail of Amelia's face, her belly, the way she stood close to Ryan like she belonged there.

Then his father's eyes filled with tears, and Ryan felt his own throat tighten.

"A grandchild," his father said, his voice thick with emotion. "What a blessing. What an incredible blessing."

Amelia glanced at Ryan, and the relief in her expression made his chest ache. She'd been so nervous, so afraid they wouldn't accept her. But his family was surrounding her with love, with welcome, with excitement.

His father took Amelia's arm gently. "Come sit down. Please. When is this baby due? We're just thrilled. Absolutely thrilled."

"Two weeks," Amelia said, letting herself be led into the family room. "January first, supposedly."

His mother pulled Ryan back, letting the others move ahead. She waited until Amelia was out of earshot before turning to him.

"Now I understand," she whispered. "Why you didn't want us to mention Sandy and Charlotte. Have you told her yet?"

"No. Tonight." Ryan's voice was low. "Mom, I didn't think I could find love again. But I love her. So much. And I can't wait for her to have this baby."

"Oh, sweetheart." His mother's eyes filled with tears

again. "I'm so happy for you. I know how hard these past three years have been."

"It's just so easy with her," Ryan said, the words tumbling out. "We get along perfectly. I knew the moment I met her there was something special about her. Something that made me feel alive again."

His mother pulled him into a tight hug. "This is a wonderful Christmas present. The best one you could have given us. Now come on, let's go rescue her from your father and brothers. I want to get to know this woman better." She pulled back and smiled through her tears. "I have a feeling she's going to be our daughter-in-law very soon."

"I hope so," Ryan said quietly. "I really hope so, Mom. I love her, and I never thought I'd be able to say that about anyone again."

Together they walked into the family room, where Amelia was already in the middle of telling the story of how they'd found each other, the hotel lobby, the Santa suit, the contractions. His family was hanging on every word, laughing and exclaiming and already falling in love with her.

Ryan stood in the doorway for a moment, just watching. His new life and his old life, finally coming together. His family, so broken by loss, beginning to heal around this woman and the promise of new life.

This was what he'd been afraid to hope for.

And now it was happening.

He just had to make sure he didn't lose it.

CHAPTER 16

The drive back to Ryan's apartment was quieter than the drive to his parents' house. Amelia stared out the window at the snow-covered streets, her mind replaying the afternoon over and over.

Ryan's family had been wonderful. More than wonderful, they'd been welcoming and warm and genuinely excited about the baby. His mother had cried happy tears and hugged her three times. His father had told stories about Ryan as a little boy that made everyone laugh. His brothers had teased him mercilessly while simultaneously making her feel like she was already part of the family.

But there had been something underneath it all. Something she couldn't quite name.

The way his mother had looked at Ryan when she thought Amelia wasn't watching, a mixture of joy and concern. The way his brother Clint had squeezed Ryan's shoulder and said, "You deserve this," like Ryan needed permission to be happy. The way his father's eyes had filled with tears when he'd said "what a blessing," like he'd been waiting a long time to say those words.

And Ryan himself had been tense all afternoon. She'd felt it in the way he held her hand, in the tightness around his eyes, in the way he kept glancing at her like he was afraid she'd disappear.

Something was going on. Something he hadn't told her.

Now, as he pulled into the parking lot of his apartment complex and cut the engine, the silence felt heavy. Weighted with words neither of them had spoken yet.

"Your family is lovely," Amelia said softly, breaking the quiet.

"They are." Ryan's hands were still on the steering wheel, his knuckles white. "They really liked you."

"I liked them too." She touched his arm. "Ryan? Is everything okay?"

He turned to look at her, and the expression on his face made her chest tighten. Pain. Raw and barely concealed.

"I need to talk to you," he said. "Inside. Where it's warm."

Fear flickered through her. "Okay."

He helped her out of the Jeep, so careful, always so careful, and guided her across the icy pavement to his door. Neither of them spoke as he unlocked the apartment, as she shrugged out of her coat and settled onto the couch.

Ryan paced to the window, stared out at the falling snow for a long moment, then turned to face her.

"There's something I need to tell you," he said. "Something I should have told you before we went to my parents' house. Before... before any of this went further."

Amelia's heart started to race. "You're scaring me."

"I don't mean to." He crossed the room and sat beside her, taking her hands in his. His palms were cold. "I just need you to understand some things about me. About my past."

"Okay," she said slowly.

Ryan took a deep breath, and when he spoke, his voice was careful, measured, like he'd rehearsed the words, but they still hurt to say.

"Three years ago, I was married."

The words hit her like a physical blow. Married. Past tense.

Amelia's throat closed. "Ryan—"

"Let me finish," he said gently. "Please. I need to get this out."

She nodded, squeezing his hands.

Taking a deep breath, he picked up her hand and held it. "Six years ago, I married my college sweetheart. We had a good life together, and about a year after we were married, she became pregnant. Our families were thrilled, and nine months later Charlotte arrived."

He picked up a glass of water and took a sip. "Sandy was a teacher at the local high school, and her students loved her. Charlotte grew, and we all doted on her. My parents and brothers adored her."

Swallowing, she could see that something was bothering him. Tears had welled in his eyes. His face had a pained expression, and she reached out and rubbed his back with her free hand.

"Sandy's mother had a stroke, and Sandy and Charlotte went to Lincoln, Montana, about eighty miles from here. It was January, and on the way home, a storm hit. They were almost to Missoula when a semi-tractor trailer lost control and spun out right in front of them."

He took a deep breath. "Sandy had nowhere to go. The semi plowed into them, causing her SUV to roll multiple times."

Amelia felt her chest ache with pain.

"I was working that evening and my ambulance was the one dispatched to the scene," he said. "I immediately recognized the car, but before I could reach them, Stan stopped me."

Tears had formed in his eyes and she wanted to hug him. This had to be bad.

"I'll never forget he looked me in the eye and said, 'Get back in the ambulance. This is not good. Let me check on her and the baby. As soon as I know, I'll come tell you. But if it's as bad as it looks, I don't want your last memory of her to be how she died.'"

Ryan took several deep breaths. "I knew they were dead. No one could survive that kind of crash. Before Stan came back, he called our captain, and he was there within ten minutes. The girls were both killed instantly."

For a moment, he took a deep breath. "I'll never forget the look on Stan's face when he came back to me. We sat there together and cried like babies. They didn't want me to see her or Charlotte. There was nothing I could do. I rode back with my captain while my ambulance took their bodies to the funeral home."

"Ryan," she said, tears streaming down her face. "I didn't know. I'm so sorry."

"I lost everything because a semi hit a patch of black ice. That's why I'm terrified of you driving to Whitefish. If I lost you and this child, I couldn't continue living. Sandy had kissed me right before they left, and I kissed Charlotte goodbye, not knowing that was the last time I would ever see them alive. So you'll have to forgive me if I don't want you to drive to Whitefish alone, if I would rather you stayed here until after the baby is born."

She bit her lip, and then she pulled him to her. This sweet man had lost so much.

"Is that her picture hanging in the hall with the young child?"

"YES. THE WORST PART," Ryan continued, his voice breaking, "was that I spent months wondering if I could have saved them. If I'd been there, if I'd been driving, would I have seen the ice? Would I have reacted faster? Could I have done something different?" He finally looked up at her, and his eyes were red-rimmed, devastated. "For a long time, I blamed myself."

"It wasn't your fault," Amelia said fiercely. "Ryan, you can't—"

"I know." He nodded. "Logically, I know. I've been to

therapy. I've worked through the guilt. But that doesn't make it easier. Doesn't make me miss them any less."

Amelia pulled one hand free and reached up to touch his face, wiping away tears she hadn't realized had fallen. "I can't imagine what you went through. What you're still going through."

"I sold the house," Ryan said. "Too many memories. I could hear Sandy calling me from the kitchen. Charlotte's laughter in the hallway. I couldn't stay there. That's why I'm in this apartment. It's temporary. Neutral. Nothing that reminds me of what I lost."

Suddenly, so many things made sense. The way he'd held her so carefully from the first moment. His terror about her driving in the snow. His insistence on keeping her safe, on being there for every moment. His fear wasn't just about becoming a father, it was about the possibility of losing another family.

"Is that why you were so desperate to find me?" Amelia asked. "After the cruise?"

Ryan nodded. "That night with you was the first time I'd felt alive since the accident. The first time I'd laughed, really laughed. The first time I'd felt like maybe I could have a future again. And when I woke up and you were gone..." He shook his head. "It felt like losing something all over again."

"I'm so sorry I didn't leave my number," Amelia whispered.

"You didn't know. How could you?" Ryan's thumb traced circles on her palm. "But when I found you in that hotel lobby, when I realized you were pregnant with my baby, it felt like... like I was being given a second chance. Like maybe the universe was telling me it wasn't over for me."

Amelia was crying openly now, her free hand pressed to her belly where their daughter was moving. "That's why you don't want me to drive to Whitefish."

"I can't lose you," Ryan said simply. "I can't lose this baby. The thought of you on those icy highways, of something happening like it happened to Sandy and Charlotte... Amelia, it terrifies me. It keeps me awake at night."

"But you said you'd drive me."

"Because I know how important it is to you to be with your family. And because if I'm driving, at least I'll be there. At least I can try to protect you." His voice broke again. "Even though I know that sometimes there's nothing you can do. Sometimes accidents just happen, and there's no one to blame and nothing you could have done differently."

Amelia shifted on the couch, awkward with her belly, and wrapped her arms around him as best she could. He buried his face in her shoulder, and she felt his body shake with silent sobs he'd probably been holding back all day.

"I've got you," she whispered, the same words he'd said to her so many times over the past few days. "I've got you."

They stayed like that for a long time, holding each other while the snow fell outside and the apartment grew dark around them. Amelia ran her fingers through his hair, pressed kisses to his temple, and let him grieve.

Finally, when his breathing had steadied and the

shaking had stopped, Ryan pulled back. His eyes were red, his face blotchy, but there was something lighter in his expression. Like a weight had been lifted.

"I should have told you sooner," he said.

"You told me when you were ready," Amelia said. "That's what matters."

"My family knows. They were there through all of it. That's why my mother cried when she saw you, it wasn't just about the baby. It was about seeing me happy again. Seeing me have a chance at the family I lost."

"They were wonderful today," Amelia said. "Your mom, your dad, your brothers, they made me feel so welcome."

"I asked them not to mention Sandy and Charlotte," Ryan admitted. "I wanted one day where you weren't being compared to her. Where this could just be about us and our baby. Was that wrong?"

"No." Amelia shook her head. "I understand why you did it. But Ryan, I would never try to replace her. Or Charlotte. They were your family. They'll always be part of your story."

"I know." He took her face in his hands. "You're not a replacement. You're something new. Something I never thought I'd have again. And this baby—" His hand moved to her belly. "This baby is a gift I don't deserve, but I'm going to treasure every single day."

"You deserve to be happy," Amelia said firmly. "You deserve love and a family and a future. What happened to Sandy and Charlotte was a tragedy, but it doesn't mean you don't get to move forward."

"I love you," Ryan said suddenly. "I know it's fast, I know we barely know each other, but Amelia, I can't imagine my life without you in it anymore."

Amelia's breath caught.

"I love you too," she whispered. "It terrifies me, and I can't imagine you not being my side, when this little one arrives.."

Ryan kissed her then, soft and gentle and full of promise. When they pulled apart, he rested his forehead against hers.

"I need to ask you something," he said.

"Okay."

"I know we haven't made all the decisions yet. But I really want to stay in Missoula. I'm asking, begging, really, for you to consider staying here. With me. Building a life here."

Amelia's heart clenched. She'd been planning to move back to Whitefish since the moment she'd been fired. Had assumed that's where she'd raise her daughter, surrounded by her parents and sisters. But that was before Ryan. Before she'd found the father of her baby and fallen in love with him. Before he asked her to marry him. Now, she just wanted to deliver her baby and then she felt like she could make the important decisions. It would be hard to be married and living separately, but she had kind of hoped he would consider moving to Whitefish. Being close to her family.

"Whitefish is two hours away," Ryan finished. "Close enough to visit regularly. Close enough that your family can be part of our daughter's life, but Amelia, I have a job here. A career. My family. And I'm asking you to give us a real chance. Not just co-parenting from different cities, but actually building something together."

The law firms in this town, were much larger than any that she'd seen in Whitefish. This would be a better place for her career. It's just that she'd been dreaming of being near her family.

She took his hand again. "I need time. We need time. To figure out what is best for the three of us."

Despite everything, the tears, the grief, the heavy conversation, Amelia found herself smiling.

"And I'm still driving you to Whitefish for Christmas," he said. "If the roads clear. If the doctor approves. I'm not letting you go alone."

"Thank you."

"But I'm staying with you until the baby arrives. I'm not leaving you to do this alone. Your family will just have to make room for one more."

Amelia laughed, the sound surprising her. "My mother is going to love you. Fair warning."

"I can handle it," Ryan said. "As long as I'm with you, I can handle anything."

And sitting there in his apartment, with his arms around her and their baby moving between them, Amelia believed him.

Maybe, just maybe, they'd found exactly what they needed in each other.

CHAPTER 17

Ryan didn't sleep.

All night long, Amelia had been having Braxton Hicks contractions. They weren't regular, not the consistent pattern that would indicate real labor, but they were frequent enough to keep him on edge. Every time she gasped or shifted uncomfortably in bed, his heart would slam against his ribs and he'd think *this is it, it's happening.*

But it wasn't. Not yet.

Still, the baby was coming soon. He could feel it in his bones, could see it in the way Amelia moved, in how low her belly had dropped. This child wasn't going to wait much longer.

And he was not going to miss his daughter's birth. No matter what.

Now Amelia knew about Sandy and Charlotte. Knew why he was terrified of icy roads and winter storms. Knew why his hands shook every time she mentioned driving to

Whitefish. But knowing his past hadn't changed her mind about going. If anything, it seemed to have made her more determined to get there before the baby came, as if she was racing against time itself.

The need to be with her family, with her mother especially, was so strong in her that it radiated off her like heat. And part of him, a small, petty part he wasn't proud of, felt jealous. This was his child, too. If anyone was going to be in that delivery room, it should be him. He should be enough.

But he knew it didn't work that way. Knew that a woman's first baby was different, that mothers and daughters shared something he couldn't understand or replicate. His own mother had told him stories about how much she'd needed her mother when he was born, how terrified she'd been until her mother arrived and told her everything would be okay.

Still. The jealousy burned.

Around five in the morning, Ryan gave up on sleep entirely. He slipped out of bed carefully, trying not to wake Amelia, and padded to the window. The first thing he noticed was the silence.

The wind had stopped.

For four days, that relentless howling had been the soundtrack to their lives together. Now, there was nothing but peaceful quiet and the soft patter of Amelia's breathing from the bedroom.

Ryan pulled back the curtain and stared out at the parking lot. The sky was beginning to lighten at the edges, that grey-blue predawn glow that came before sunrise. And there, just visible on the horizon, was a break in the clouds. A promise of clear skies.

The storm had passed.

Which meant the road crews would be out soon. Meant the highways would be cleared. Meant there was no reason, no excuse, to keep Amelia here in Missoula where she was safe.

Tomorrow was Christmas Eve. She'd made it clear she wanted to be in Whitefish with her family. And as much as he loved her, God, he loved her so much it terrified him, she was indeed one of the most stubborn women he'd ever met.

But if that was her only fault, he could live with it. He'd learned long ago that the people you loved came with rough edges and quirks and things that drove you crazy. Sandy had been chronically late to everything, and it had made him insane, but he'd loved her anyway.

Though Amelia would need to learn that when he put his foot down about something important, she needed to listen. He wasn't trying to control her, he just wanted to keep her safe. There was a difference.

This time, though, he couldn't force her to stay. Wouldn't force her. And he would never, ever let her make that drive alone.

His phone buzzed on the kitchen counter, and he grabbed it before the sound could wake Amelia.

Mom flashed on the screen.

"Hello?" he said quietly, moving into the kitchen.

"Did you tell her?" His mother didn't bother with pleasantries. "About Sandy and Charlotte?"

"Yes, Mom."

"How did she take it?"

Ryan closed his eyes, remembering the way Amelia had cried with him. The way she'd held him while he fell apart. The way she hadn't tried to fix it or make it better, just let him grieve.

"We both cried," he said. "Talked about how unfair it was. She understands now why I don't want her on those roads. But I don't think I convinced her not to go to Whitefish."

His mother sighed. "Then you should take her, sweetheart. You've got that Jeep that can handle anything. I know I'll be worried sick about all three of you, but this is her first child. She's afraid." Her voice softened. "I remember how much I wanted my mother there when I had you. How terrified I was until she walked into that hospital room and held my hand."

Ryan leaned against the counter, his free hand gripping the edge. "Mom, I'm terrified of another accident. What if—"

"Lightning doesn't strike twice, baby."

"It could." His voice came out harsh. "You know it could. I see accidents every day. Good people, careful people, doing everything right and still ending up—" He couldn't finish the sentence.

"I know." His mother's voice was thick with unshed tears. "But you can't live your life in fear. You can't keep her locked up just because you're afraid of what might happen. That's not love, Ryan. That's prison."

The words hit him like a slap. "I'm not trying to—"

"I know you're not. I know you love her and you want to protect her. But don't let her go alone. That baby has dropped and is in position. It's just a matter of time before she arrives."

Ryan pressed his fingers against his eyes, willing away the burn of tears. "What if she goes into labor while we're on the road?"

"Then you pull over and deliver your own child." His mother's voice was firm now, practical. "You're a paramedic, Ryan. You know how to do this. You've done it before."

He had. Three times in his career, women who'd waited too long or whose labor had come on so fast there was no time to get to the hospital. It was terrifying and joyous in equal measure, and he'd loved helping those babies enter the world. But those hadn't been his babies. Hadn't been his Amelia lying there vulnerable and in pain.

"I can deliver a baby," he said quietly. "But what if there are complications? What if she has a medical emergency and we're stuck on some highway in the middle of nowhere? Mom, I can't lose them. I can't go through that again."

Silence stretched between them, heavy and aching.

"You said you love her," his mother finally said.

"I do." The words came out raw. "God, I love her so much."

"Then sometimes we have to do things that terrify us to make the people we love happy. Your logic is telling you to keep her here where it's safe. But your heart, your heart knows that keeping her from her family when she needs them most would hurt her. Would hurt your relationship."

Ryan swallowed hard. "You're supposed to be on my side."

"I am on your side, sweetheart. That's why I'm telling you this." She paused. "We'll miss you at Christmas. So much. But you have to do this for Amelia. And you have to trust that everything will be okay."

He wanted to argue. Wanted to tell his mother no, that he'd made up his mind and Amelia would just have to deal with it. But he knew he was wrong. Knew that forcing Amelia to stay would be the beginning of the end of whatever they were building together.

"I'll let you know when we get there," he said finally, his voice defeated.

"I love you, son."

"Love you too, Mom."

He disconnected the call and set the phone down, then braced his hands on the counter and dropped his head. His whole body felt heavy, weighed down by fear and resignation and a bone-deep exhaustion that had nothing to do with lack of sleep.

"Was that your mom?"

Ryan's head jerked up. Amelia stood in the doorway, her hair sleep-mussed, wearing one of his old sweatshirts that stretched tight across her belly. She looked beautiful and fragile and so damn pregnant that his heart clenched.

"Yes," he managed.

"I hope you told her how much I enjoyed yesterday." She moved into the kitchen, her hand on the small of her back, the way she always did now when she walked.

"I didn't, but you can call her later." He turned to the coffee maker, needing something to do with his hands. Something normal and routine that didn't involve thinking about icy highways and semi-trucks and losing everything that mattered.

This morning, nervousness crawled under his skin like ants. Fear sat in his stomach like a stone.

"Did you see the sun is shining?" Amelia's face was lit up with joy, with hope, with an excitement that made him feel like the world's biggest asshole for wanting to crush it.

"Yes," he said flatly. "I saw."

If only Mother Nature had given him a few more days. If only the storm had lasted through Christmas. Then he could have kept her here, kept her safe, and she would have had no choice but to accept it.

"How long will it take them to clear the roads?" she asked, accepting the coffee mug he handed her.

"I don't know." He couldn't look at her. Couldn't see that happiness knowing what he had to do. "Are you still determined to get to Whitefish?"

"Yes." There was steel in her voice. "It's my family, Ryan. I want to be there with them. I understand why you're hesitant, really, I do. And I would feel so much better if you came with me. But if you don't want to go, I understand. I'm leaving in the morning either way. I'll give the road department today to finish clearing, but tomorrow morning, I'm headed to Whitefish."

There it was. The ultimatum he'd been dreading. With or without him, she was going.

"You know," he said, turning to face her, "I think we're having our first argument."

She smiled, actually smiled, like this was amusing instead of terrifying. "No, I'm not going to fight with you. I understand why you feel the way you do. But I'm going home, Ryan."

"And there's that stubborn streak of yours." He couldn't keep the edge out of his voice.

"Not stubborn. Determined." She set down her coffee mug and moved closer, her hand finding his chest, right over his heart. "This baby is going to be born surrounded by my family. My mother especially. And you, I hope. But I understand if that's too hard for you."

She was giving him an out. Telling him he could stay here in Missoula, safe and sound, while she drove two hours on icy roads to Whitefish. While she risked her life and their baby's life because she needed her mother.

The thought of her making that drive alone made him physically ill.

Ryan took a deep breath and felt the fight drain out of him. He'd lost this battle before it had even begun. His mother was right, he couldn't keep Amelia here against her will. Couldn't let fear control his life or poison what they were building together.

"You're not going anywhere without me," he said quietly. "Ever. So as much as I disagree with this decision, I'll take you to Whitefish. We'll leave at nine in the morning. Give the roads time to thaw in the sun."

Amelia's face transformed. She clapped her hands together like a child, bouncing slightly on her toes, or as much as she could bounce at nine months pregnant. "I can't wait! I'm so excited. It's going to be a wonderful Christmas."

Ryan pulled her into his arms, careful of her belly, and buried his face in her hair. She smelled like his shampoo and something floral and uniquely her. He breathed her in, memorizing the moment.

Please, he prayed to whatever God or universe might be listening. Please let us make it there safely. Please don't take them from me. I can't survive losing another family.

"I love you," he whispered against her temple.

Amelia pulled back to look at him, her eyes soft. "I love you too."

"Then promise me something."

"What?"

"Promise me you'll do exactly what I say if anything goes wrong on that drive. No arguing, no questioning. If I tell you to do something, you do it immediately."

Something in his tone must have conveyed how serious he was, because her expression sobered. "I promise."

"Okay." He kissed her forehead, then her nose, then her lips. "Then let's get you home for Christmas."

Even if it killed him.

CHAPTER 18

The roads were treacherous.

Even with Ryan's steady hands on the wheel and the Jeep's four-wheel drive gripping the pavement, Amelia could feel every slide, every moment when the tires struggled for purchase on ice hidden beneath a thin layer of melting snow. The highway crews had done their job, but nature didn't give up its grip easily. Not in Montana. Not in December.

"Thank you for coming home with me," she said, her hand resting on her belly where their daughter was doing somersaults. "I know how hard this is for you. I'm so grateful you're here."

"Are you feeling all right?" Ryan's eyes never left the road, his jaw tight with concentration.

"Yes. My feet are swelling, but that's just from sitting. As soon as we get there, I'll put them up." She didn't mention the cramping that had started an hour ago. Didn't mention the pressure low in her pelvis that was becoming harder to ignore.

"Are your folks going to be okay with us being together?" Ryan asked. "The whole showing up pregnant and unmarried thing?"

Amelia laughed, though it came out more nervous than she'd intended. "What more can happen? I'm already pregnant. It's not like I can get more knocked up."

Ryan's lips twitched despite the tension in his shoulders. "Fair point."

"I think they're going to love you," she said, and she meant it. How could they not? This man had driven through dangerous roads because she'd needed him to. This man had opened his heart to her after losing everything. This man loved their daughter before he'd even met her.

She loved him. God, she loved him so much it terrified her.

He'd told her he loved Sandy, had probably sworn forever to her too, and look how that had ended, it still hurt. Made her wonder if maybe she was too stubborn, too difficult, too much for him to truly want forever with.

After all, she'd practically coerced him into making this drive.

Her parents would love him, she was almost certain. But as for him sleeping in her room with her, unmarried, under their roof? That might cause some tension. Her father was traditional that way. Her mother, too, though she had a softer edge about it.

This morning, she'd lost her mucus plug. She'd been in the bathroom when it happened, and she'd stared at the evidence for a long moment before carefully not mentioning it to Ryan. According to everything she'd read, labor would start within one to three days.

If she'd told him, they never would have left Missoula.

All morning, she'd felt giddy and anxious in equal measure. Soon, maybe today, maybe tomorrow, she'd meet her daughter. Soon, her family would know her secret. Soon, everything would change.

"We're thirty minutes out," Ryan said, breaking into her thoughts.

Thirty minutes. Half an hour until she had to face her parents and sisters and tell them the truth she'd been hiding for nine months. Until she had to see their faces when they realized their golden child had fallen spectacularly from grace.

Never in her life had she done something her parents disapproved of. She'd been the perfect daughter, straight A's, full scholarship, prestigious career, everything they'd hoped for and more. And now here she was, pregnant and unemployed and in love with a man she'd known for less than a week total.

They would love her anyway. She knew that. The Millers loved their children unconditionally. But the disappointment would be there, at least at first, and that made her stomach twist with anxiety.

And what was her mother's secret? The mysterious reason she'd insisted everyone come home for Christmas?

All year, her mother had been quiet about something, and Amelia feared it was something terrible. Cancer. Heart disease. Something that meant they were losing time.

The thought made her chest tight.

As they entered the Whitefish town limits, Amelia felt her anxiety spike. Everything looked the same, the same gas station where she'd gotten her first speeding ticket, the same coffee shop where she'd studied for the bar exam, the same buildings she'd grown up seeing every day.

But she was different. Changed. And in a few minutes, everyone would see just how much.

Ryan slowed at an intersection, and suddenly a massive semi-truck barreled through the red light, missing them by what couldn't have been more than ten feet. The Jeep rocked with the force of displaced air.

Amelia's heart stopped.

She looked at Ryan and saw him go white, his hands locked on the steering wheel so tightly his knuckles were bloodless. She could see it all playing out in his mind, the truck, the ice, Sandy and Charlotte—

"We're fine," she said quickly, reaching out to touch his arm. "Ryan, we're fine. You kept us safe. You're an amazing driver."

His jaw worked, muscles jumping beneath his skin. "Bad things can happen to anyone. Even the golden child."

The words were meant lightly, but she could hear the fear beneath them. The barely controlled terror of a man who'd lost everything once and was desperately trying not to lose it again.

"Not with you by my side," Amelia said firmly, rubbing her hand up and down his forearm, feeling the tension there. "You'll take good care of me and our daughter. You already have been."

He glanced at her, and something in his expression softened. "I'll do my best."

"That's all I could ever ask for."

They drove through the intersection, slowly, carefully, and turned onto her street. Maple Avenue. The street where she'd learned to ride a bike, where she'd had her first kiss, where she'd left from to go to college and then law school and then her life in Cheyenne.

Coming back felt like stepping into a memory that had been waiting for her all along.

"That house," she said, pointing to the two-story colonial with the wraparound porch. "The one with the blue shutters."

Her childhood home. The place where she'd always felt safe.

The driveway was empty except for her parents' sedan.

"Looks like no one else is here yet," she observed, relief flooding through her. That would give her parents time to absorb the shock before Emma and Olivia showed up and made everything more chaotic.

Ryan put the Jeep in park and turned off the engine. The sudden silence felt heavy, weighted with anticipation.

"Let me help you," he said. "The sidewalk looks clear, but I'm not taking any chances. Not after—" He didn't finish the sentence.

This man. This beautiful, broken, careful man who loved so hard it hurt him.

Amelia reached over and grabbed his face with both hands, pulling him toward her. She kissed him thoroughly, deeply, trying to pour every ounce of love and gratitude and promise into that single moment.

When they finally broke apart, both breathing hard, Ryan smiled at her. "I needed that."

"And I need you," she said simply. "Every day. For the rest of my life."

He climbed out and came around to her door, opening it and offering his hand. "Soon you won't have to help me get out of cars," she said. "I'll be able to do it myself again."

His eyebrows rose. "In a couple weeks, maybe."

"Nope." She took his hand and let him help her down, her feet finding the cleared pavement. "I lost my mucus plug this morning. Labor should happen in the next day or two."

Ryan froze. "You what?"

"Lost my mucus plug. It's one of the signs that labor is—"

"I know what it means!" His voice rose, and then he seemed to catch himself, glancing around at the quiet neighborhood before lowering his volume. "Why the hell didn't you tell me before we left?"

"Because you wouldn't have brought me to Whitefish," Amelia said calmly. "And I needed to be here. With my family."

He stared at her, and she could see about five different

emotions warring on his face, anger, fear, frustration, resignation, and underneath it all, reluctant admiration.

"You are one stubborn, manipulative, impossible woman," he said finally.

"Determined," she corrected. "The word you're looking for is determined."

"That's not the word I'm looking for."

Amelia stepped closer, as close as her belly would allow, and looked up at him. "And I hope and pray you love me anyway. All of me. Even the stubborn parts. Especially the stubborn parts."

Ryan's expression softened. He reached up and cupped her face, his thumb brushing across her cheekbone. "I love you, Amelia Miller. I love you so much it scares me. I love our child. And I'm going to talk to your father about us getting married as soon as possible."

Joy exploded in her chest, so sudden and overwhelming that tears sprang to her eyes. "Really?"

"Really." He smiled, and it was the first genuine, unguarded smile she'd seen since they'd started this drive. "I love you. I've loved you since that night on the cruise. Since you walked away without leaving your number and I thought I'd lost the best thing that ever happened to me." His voice dropped to a whisper. "Please don't ever leave me again."

"Never," Amelia promised, and she meant it with every fiber of her being. "You're stuck with me now. Forever."

"Forever," he repeated, like he was testing the word, seeing if it would break under the weight of his past. When it didn't, he smiled wider. "Okay then. Let's go tell your family they're about to become grandparents."

He took her arm and guided her up the walkway, slowly, carefully, like she was made of glass. The front steps had been salted and shoveled clean, and she could see Christmas lights twinkling in the window.

Before they reached the porch, the front door flew open.

Her mother stood there, backlit by the warm glow of the house, and for a moment she just stared. Then her hand flew to her mouth.

"Amelia? Oh my God, honey—" Her mother's gaze traveled down, landing on Amelia's obvious belly, and her eyes went wide. "Why didn't you tell us?"

Amelia felt Ryan's hand tighten on her arm, steadying her. "It's a long, complicated story, Mom. But first, I want you to meet my fiancé." She felt Ryan startle slightly at the word, but he didn't correct her. "And before you get upset with him for not marrying me before now, you have to hear our story."

Her mother's expression shifted from shock to something that looked suspiciously like mama-bear protectiveness. She fixed Ryan with a look that could have melted steel. "Come in, young man. I hope you two have a very good explanation for this."

Amelia and Ryan exchanged a glance, and despite everything, the fear, the anxiety, the uncertainty, she felt laughter bubble up in her chest.

"You're not going to believe it when we tell you," Amelia

said. "But because of a blizzard and a broken condom and the worst storm Missoula has seen in years, we found each other again."

"And she's not getting away this time," Ryan added, looking down at her with such fierce love in his eyes that it made her breathless. "Not ever."

Her mother's expression softened slightly. "Well, don't just stand there in the cold. Come inside before you both freeze."

They stepped into the warmth of her childhood home, and Amelia breathed in the familiar scents, her mother's cinnamon candles, the pine garland draped over the banister, something baking in the kitchen that smelled like home.

Her father appeared from the living room, newspaper still in hand, and stopped dead when he saw her. "Amelia? We weren't expecting you until—" His gaze dropped to her belly, and his mouth fell open. "Oh."

"Hi, Daddy," Amelia said, suddenly feeling like she was sixteen again and had just been caught sneaking in past curfew. "Surprise?"

Her father looked at Ryan, then at her belly, then at Ryan again. "Who's this?"

"This is Ryan Allen," Amelia said. "He's a paramedic in Missoula. He's my fiancé. And he's the father of your grandchild, who should be making an appearance in the next day or two."

The silence that followed was deafening.

Then her mother started crying. Her father sank down

onto the bottom step like his legs wouldn't hold him anymore. And somewhere upstairs, Amelia heard a door open and footsteps pounding down the hallway.

"Did someone say baby?" Emma's voice called out. "Amelia, is that you?"

Within seconds, both her sisters were thundering down the stairs. Emma reached the bottom first, took one look at Amelia's belly, and screamed. Olivia was right behind her, and her jaw literally dropped.

"Holy shit," Olivia breathed. "The golden child is pregnant?"

"Language," their mother said automatically, still crying.

"But she's, you're—" Emma seemed unable to form complete sentences. She looked at Ryan. "Who are you?"

"This is chaos," Ryan murmured in Amelia's ear. "Is it always like this?"

"Always," Amelia confirmed. "Welcome to the Miller family."

Her father finally stood, crossed to where they were standing, and extended his hand to Ryan. "Brent Miller. I assume you're the father?"

"Yes, sir," Ryan said, shaking his hand firmly. "Ryan Allen. And I know this isn't how things should have happened, but I love your daughter very much. And I'd like your permission to marry her."

Her father studied Ryan for a long moment, and Amelia held her breath.

Then her father smiled, actually smiled. "Well, you've got guts, I'll give you that. Coming here, meeting us like this." He glanced at Amelia. "And if my daughter loves you, which I'm assuming she does, given the circumstances, then I suppose we'd better start planning a wedding. Though it might have to wait until after the baby comes."

"Definitely after," Amelia said, feeling a cramp roll through her abdomen. She tried to hide it, but Ryan noticed immediately.

"Was that a contraction?" he asked, his hand going to her lower back.

"Maybe? I don't know. It could just be Braxton Hicks."

"How far apart are they?"

"I don't know, I haven't been timing—"

Another cramp hit, stronger this time, and Amelia gasped, her hand flying to her belly.

"Okay," Ryan said, his paramedic voice clicking into place. "We need to get you sitting down. Mrs. Miller, do you have a comfortable chair where she can put her feet up?"

"The recliner in the living room," her mother said immediately, all traces of tears gone, replaced by practical maternal efficiency. "Brent, help Ryan get her settled. Emma, get pillows. Olivia, time her contractions. I'll call the hospital and let them know we might be coming in."

As her family swarmed around her, as Ryan guided her to the living room with steady hands and worried eyes, as her mother barked orders and her sisters scrambled to help, Amelia felt something settle in her chest.

This was home. Not just the house, but this, family

surrounding her, chaos and love and people who would show up when it mattered most.

And Ryan was part of it now. Part of her family. Part of her future.

"I love you," she told him as he helped her into the recliner.

"I love you too," he said, kneeling beside her. "And I'm not leaving your side. Not for anything."

"Promise?"

"Promise. You're stuck with me now. Forever."

Forever. The word didn't scare her anymore.

It sounded like the best Christmas present she'd ever received.

CHAPTER 19

*N*oah Mitchell stood at the rental car counter in Missoula Regional Airport, his jaw clenched so tight it ached, and tried very hard not to lose his temper with the woman behind the computer screen.

He refused to let her ruin this trip. He absolutely refused.

For the first time in five years, five long, complicated years, he was going to spend Christmas with his father. His father and the new wife Noah had never met. After everything they'd been through with his mother, after all the chaos and dysfunction and barely controlled madness that had defined his childhood, his father finally seemed happy.

Noah wanted to be there. Needed to be there. Needed to see with his own eyes that his father had found some measure of peace.

"I specifically rented a four-wheel drive vehicle in case of bad weather," Noah said, keeping his voice level through sheer force of will. "I understand Montana winters. That's why I made arrangements ahead of time."

The rental agent, Stacy, according to her name tag, looked at him with the patient expression of someone who'd had this conversation twenty times already today. "Sir, I understand your frustration. Your vehicle is ready and waiting. But what I'm trying to tell you is that you cannot leave Missoula. The highway between here and Whitefish is closed. Not just inadvisable, closed. As in gates down and locked."

She slid a piece of paper across the counter with a hotel name and phone number written on it. "I strongly suggest you call this hotel right now and book a room before they sell out completely."

Noah stared at her, trying to process the words. Closed? How could they close an entire highway before a storm even started? And hotel rooms selling out, that happened for concerts or conventions, not snowstorms.

"What do you mean, sell out?" Even to his own ears, his voice sounded incredulous.

Stacy's expression shifted from patient to concerned. "Sir, the biggest storm of the decade is expected to hit in the next few hours. Right now, there are still a few hotel rooms available in Missoula. In about an hour, this city is going to be flooded with stranded travelers, and there won't be anything left." She paused. "You can take your vehicle if you want, but you won't get out of town. The highway patrol isn't letting anyone through."

She was talking to him, a doctor, someone with an

M.D. after his name, someone who'd survived medical school and residency, like he was an idiot who couldn't understand basic cause and effect.

And maybe he was being an idiot. Maybe growing up in Houston, where winter meant putting on a light jacket, had left him completely unprepared for the reality of Montana in December.

This was supposed to be his first Christmas with his father since the old man had remarried. The first Christmas that felt like it might actually be pleasant instead of a minefield of his mother's unpredictable moods. He'd been looking forward to it for months.

"Noah."

He turned to find Hannah already on her phone, stepping away from the counter to make a call. Of course, she was. While he stood there arguing with reality, his best friend was already solving the problem.

This was why they worked so well together. Noah got caught up in the details, in what should be happening versus what was actually happening. Hannah just rolled with whatever came at them and found solutions.

He watched her talk on the phone, watched her blonde hair catch the fluorescent lights, watched the way she gestured with one hand while holding her phone with the other, watched her laugh at something the person on the other end said.

Six years. They'd been friends for six years. Partners. Study buddies in medical school, support systems during residency, and now colleagues at one of Houston's busiest emergency rooms. And in all that time, he'd never crossed the line from friendship to something more.

Even though he'd wanted to. God, how he'd wanted to.

"Yes, ma'am," Hannah was saying into her phone. "We just landed at the airport, and the rental agency is telling us we need to find a hotel room immediately. Do you have anything available?"

She paused, listening, and then she started laughing, that bright, genuine laugh that always made something in Noah's chest feel lighter.

"All right, we'll take it. Let me give you a credit card number to hold the reservation." She rattled off numbers from memory. "Perfect. We'll be there as soon as we leave the airport. Thank you so much."

She ended the call and turned back to him, triumphant. "Done. Got us a room."

"Thank you," Noah said to Stacy, who looked relieved that at least one of them was being reasonable.

Hannah grabbed his arm and steered him away from the counter. Behind them, Noah could see a long line of increasingly anxious travelers waiting to rent vehicles, all of them probably about to get the same news he'd just received.

Maybe he should be grateful they had a Jeep and, apparently, a hotel room. Maybe fighting reality wasn't the best use of his energy.

"When we get the vehicle, I want you to check the local news websites," Noah said as they walked toward the exit. "Verify that the roads are actually closed. I still can't believe they'd shut down a major highway before the storm even hits."

Hannah stopped walking and turned to face him, one eyebrow raised in that expression he knew meant she thought he was being ridiculous. "Noah. You've never lived anywhere that gets real snowstorms. In Wyoming, where I grew up, remember?—they have actual gates that lock across the roads. Not suggestions. Not warnings. Physical barriers. Because people like you, intelligent, educated, stubborn people, would absolutely try to drive through blizzards and then need to be rescued."

"I wouldn't—"

"You would," she said flatly. "You're doing it right now. You're literally planning to double-check the news reports because you don't believe what multiple people have told you."

Noah opened his mouth to argue, then closed it again. She was right. Of course she was right.

"I just wanted to get to Whitefish," he said quietly. "I wanted to see my dad. Meet his new wife. It's been so long since we've spent real time together. Since before Mom—" He couldn't finish that sentence either.

Hannah's expression softened. She reached out and squeezed his arm. "I know. And we will get there. Just maybe not today."

They found their rental Jeep in the lot and loaded their suitcases. The sky above them was grey and heavy, the kind of grey that promised snow and lots of it. The temperature had dropped significantly since they'd landed thirty minutes ago.

Noah was grateful Hannah had agreed to come with him on this trip. She didn't have family to visit for Christmas, her parents had retired to Arizona and were on a cruise, and when he'd mentioned his plans, she'd offered to tag along for moral support.

"Meeting the new stepmother seems like it might be stressful," she'd said. "You might need backup."

She'd been joking, but she wasn't wrong. His father's happiness was wonderful, but it also meant Noah had to navigate a new family dynamic, had to figure out where he fit in this new configuration. Having Hannah there would make it easier. She made everything easier.

As they climbed into the Jeep, Hannah already had her phone out, pulling up the Montana Department of Transportation website. "Yep. All highways between Missoula and Whitefish: closed due to severe weather and blowing snow. The storm is already hitting the northern part of the state." She looked up at him. "We're officially stuck. But hey, at least I got us a room."

"How many rooms?" Noah asked, starting the engine.

"One." Hannah didn't look up from her phone. "That was all they had left. I had to give them a credit card number immediately to hold it, or it would've been gone before we got there."

One room.

They'd been friends for six years and had never shared a room. Never even come close. There had been an unspoken boundary between them, a line neither of them had crossed because crossing it would change everything.

And Noah had spent six years very carefully not changing anything.

He'd watched his parents destroy each other. Both doctors. Both brilliant. Both so consumed by their work and their egos and their need to be right that they'd created a home that felt more like a war zone than a family.

His mother especially. She'd been what the psychiatrists had eventually called "psychotic with narcissistic features." However, that clinical diagnosis didn't begin to capture what it was like to grow up in the crossfire of her mood swings and delusions.

Noah had learned early that relationships between doctors were dangerous. That working together and sleeping together created a toxic mixture of competition and resentment. That loving someone you also had to professionally respect was a recipe for disaster.

So he'd kept things with Hannah firmly in the friend zone. Even when he wanted more. Even when he caught himself staring at her across the ER, admiring the way she handled patients, the way she made split-second decisions that saved lives. Even when he went out with other women and found himself comparing them all to Hannah and finding them lacking.

He drove through the small mountain town, following the GPS directions to the hotel Hannah had booked. The snowflakes were starting to fall now, just a few at first, then more, then suddenly so many that it was like someone had torn open a pillow and dumped the contents from the sky.

"I think snow-mageddon has arrived," Noah said, watching the flakes swirl in his headlights.

"And you wanted to drive to Whitefish in this," Hannah said, shaking her head. "Yeah, that would've gone well."

"Point taken."

They pulled up under the hotel awning just as the storm kicked into high gear. Through the windshield, Noah could barely see the building in front of them.

"Let me get the suitcases," Hannah said, already climbing out. "You park the car."

But when they walked into the lobby, the frazzled clerk behind the desk looked at them with an expression somewhere between relief and panic.

"You must be Dr. Reeves," she said to Hannah. "Thank God you're here. The manager wanted to give your room away to someone else, and I told him it was already reserved. But we're completely full now. The only room we have available is the honeymoon suite. Is that... is that okay?"

Noah felt his stomach drop. The honeymoon suite. Of course it was.

"You don't have anything else?" he asked, hearing the edge in his voice. "Two rooms? Two beds?"

"Sir, you're lucky to still have this room," the clerk said. "We've been sold out for the past hour. People are sleeping in the lobby."

Hannah laughed, that same easy laugh that meant she

found the whole situation amusing instead of catastrophic. "We'll take it. And all the perks that come with it."

The clerk smiled with visible relief and quickly made key cards. "Wonderful. Tonight we'll bring up chocolate-covered strawberries and champagne. It's all included in the honeymoon package."

Perfect. Exactly what they didn't need.

They took the elevator to the third floor, neither of them speaking. Noah could feel tension radiating off his own body, could feel his carefully maintained boundaries starting to crack.

He opened the door to the suite and stopped dead.

It was exactly what he'd feared. A king-sized bed with rose petals scattered across the comforter. Dim lighting designed for romance. A heart-shaped jacuzzi tub visible through an open bathroom door. Mirrors on the ceiling. Champagne already chilling in an ice bucket.

A love playground.

"What the hell," Noah breathed. "We can't stay here."

Hannah walked past him into the room, setting down her suitcase and looking around with undisguised amusement. She touched the rose petals on the bed, then walked over to examine the jacuzzi.

"Why not?" she said, turning to grin at him. "I think this looks like fun. Besides, what choice do we have? Sleep in the lobby?"

Noah stared at her, trying to read her expression. Was she serious? Was this actually not bothering her at all?

"Go move the car from under the awning," Hannah said,

already unzipping her suitcase. "I'll unpack while you're gone. Get us settled."

He fled.

It took him ten minutes to find a parking spot in the increasingly packed lot, and by the time he jogged back to the hotel, the storm had turned into a complete whiteout. He could barely see five feet in front of him. Snow was already piling up in drifts against the building.

They weren't going anywhere. Not tonight. Probably not tomorrow either.

Noah stood in the hallway outside the honeymoon suite for a long moment, trying to calm his racing heart, trying to convince himself that this was fine. They were adults. They were professionals. They could share a room for one night without it meaning anything.

He unlocked the door and stepped inside.

And froze.

Hannah was in the jacuzzi. Naked, or at least, he had to assume she was naked beneath the thick layer of bubbles that covered her from neck to toes. Her blonde hair was piled on top of her head, a few strands escaping to curl against her neck. Her head was tilted back against the edge of the tub, her eyes closed, her skin flushed from the heat.

She looked like every fantasy he'd spent six years trying not to have.

"Oh good, you're back," Hannah said, opening her eyes and smiling at him. "Come on in. The water is perfect. And look—" She gestured to the side of the tub where two champagne flutes sat next to a plate of chocolate-covered strawberries. "They already delivered the perks."

Noah swallowed hard. His mouth had gone completely dry. "Hannah—"

"Noah." She sat up slightly, and he quickly averted his eyes, afraid of what he might see. "We're stuck here. In a snowstorm. In a honeymoon suite. We might as well enjoy it, right?"

"We're friends," he said, the words coming out hoarse. "Colleagues."

"I know." Her voice was soft now, serious. "But maybe we could be more than that. If you wanted to be."

His heart was pounding so hard he could hear it in his ears. "If I get in that tub with you—"

"Then everything changes," Hannah finished. "I know. But Noah, maybe it's time for things to change. Maybe we've been holding back for long enough."

He stared at her, at the invitation in her eyes, at six years of carefully maintained boundaries hovering on the edge of collapse.

And for the first time in his adult life, Noah stopped overthinking and just felt.

"Okay," he said.

All I Want for Christmas
Available Everywhere

All I want for
Christmas
USA TODAY BESTSELLING AUTHOR
SYLVIA MCDANIEL

THE RELUCTANT SANTA

"His soul is mine."

Devon spoke the words with quiet certainty, watching the humans gathered in the sales office below. They were completely oblivious to his presence, as they always were. One of the best things about being a fallen angel, though he'd never admit to missing heaven, was the ability to observe mortals like watching actors on a stage. Sometimes he even got to direct the show.

A chill wind howled outside the downtown Denver high-rise, rattling the windows and heralding winter's arrival. December. The holiday season. The perfect time to increase his soul count. Humans became so predictably desperate this time of year, desperate for love, for meaning, for connection. And desperation made them vulnerable.

Devon studied his next target carefully. Brown hair, expressive eyebrows, a quirky grin that probably charmed clients into signing contracts they'd regret later. Colin McDermott. Thirty-two years old. Sales director at a tech startup. No wife. No girlfriend. No meaningful relationships of any kind, just work, ambition, and an insatiable hunger for more money.

Perfect.

The man's life meter was about to expire unless he made drastic changes. And Devon had no intention of letting those changes happen.

"Devon."

The voice echoed through the atmosphere before the being who irritated him most materialized in his peripheral vision. He didn't need to turn his head to know who it was. He'd recognize that sanctimonious tone anywhere.

"Doing a soul count before he's even yours?" Gabriella's voice held amusement. "That's awfully presumptuous."

Devon kept his eyes on Colin as the angel fully shimmered into existence beside him. He could feel her presence like static electricity, all that nauseating righteousness radiating off her in waves.

When he finally glanced her way, his carefully maintained indifference faltered.

Gone were the flowing white robes he associated with heaven's agents. Instead, Gabriella wore white leather—a jacket that hugged her frame, pants that disappeared into white knee-high boots. A gold belt cinched her waist, holding a cross that marked her rank: sergeant, angel first class. Even her halo had attitude, tilted at a rakish angle that suggested she knew exactly how good she looked.

In mortal terms, she was absolutely stunning.

"Whoever's in charge of your wardrobe, I like the changes they've made," Devon said, letting his gaze travel the length of her before a searing heat—a warning from above—reminded him he was crossing boundaries. He forced his eyes away. "Please tell me they've ditched those boring robes permanently."

Gabriella tossed her blonde hair, her blue eyes flashing with something that made them glint silver. "My robes are hardly boring. But no, one of my cases is a motorcyclist. I'm riding shotgun today, trying to keep him from becoming a stain on I-25. The robes kept billowing up and blocking my view." She gestured to her outfit. "I found a more practical solution."

"Practical." Devon shook his head and forced himself to focus on Colin, who was currently charming a client with that easy smile that hid his complete lack of empathy. "I thought your promotion last Easter moved you out of the guardian angel division. Shouldn't you be managing other angels instead of doing fieldwork?"

"We all pitch in during the holidays," Gabriella said, her voice taking on that patient, instructive tone that made Devon want to snap at her. "You know how it works. Soul quotas increase. Competition intensifies. Only the strongest survive."

She moved closer, studying Colin with an expression Devon couldn't quite read. "Besides, every time I go up against you, I lose souls I should have saved. I'm not letting that happen this time. Colin McDermott belongs to heaven, not hell."

Devon felt his jaw tighten. "He's a selfish, greedy man with no meaningful relationships and a heart made of stone. Look at him down there, he just convinced that client to sign a contract he knows will bankrupt the man's company within six months. Colin doesn't care. All he sees are his commission numbers."

"He's lost," Gabriella countered. "There's a difference. He just needs someone to show him there's more to life than money and success."

"His time is about to expire," Devon said flatly. "I'm here to collect what's owed."

"Maybe." Gabriella's voice softened, and when he looked at her, he saw something like pity in her expression. "Or maybe I can give him guidance. Help him choose a different path before it's too late."

"Not this time." Devon smiled, but there was no warmth in it. "Heavenly angels may not be able to play dirty, but I can. And I intend to win this one."

Gabriella laughed, a sound like bells that made something uncomfortable twist in Devon's chest. "Always so arrogant. You know what they say about pride, don't you?"

"It's what got me where I am," Devon shot back. "So yes, I'm familiar with the concept."

She studied him for a long moment, her expression shifting from amusement to something more serious. "Playing dirty is exactly what landed you in purgatory patrol in the first place, Devon. Why would I expect anything different now?"

The words hit harder than they should have. Devon felt his hands curl into fists at his sides, frustration spiraling through him like smoke. How he'd fallen, the choices he'd made, the rules he'd broken, none of that mattered anymore. He'd been given a role in the cosmic bureaucracy, and he played it well.

"How I got here doesn't matter," he said, keeping his voice level. "I need this soul. You understand quotas, Gabriella. Make your numbers or get sent back to the pit to fight and claw your way out for another chance. I'm not going back there."

"And Colin McDermott deserves to be saved," Gabriella replied, turning back to watch the human below. Her voice gentled. "Look at him. He has no idea his priorities are destroying him. He's selfish and greedy because he's never been loved. Because no one's ever shown him there's another way to live."

"Love." Devon practically spat the word. "You heavenly angels think love solves everything. That all a person needs is to feel warm and fuzzy inside, and suddenly they'll stop being terrible."

"Love changes people," Gabriella said quietly. "Even you deserved to be loved once, Devon. If I had been your guardian angel, I would have found someone to show you what that felt like. Maybe then you would have made different choices."

The words landed like a blow to the solar plexus. For a moment, just a moment, Devon allowed himself to remember what it had been like before. Before the fall. Before the bitterness. When he'd believed in redemption and second chances and all the things Gabriella still fought for.

Then he shoved the memory down where it belonged.

"Well, you weren't my angel," he said coldly. "And now I'm the big man's soul collector. That's the role I play."

"But why?" Gabriella turned to face him fully, and the genuine confusion in her eyes made him want to look away. "Why would you want to drag more souls into the darkness you're already trapped in? Don't you get tired of it, Devon? The lies, the manipulation, the endless cycle of corruption?"

Devon clenched his jaw so hard he thought his teeth might crack. Hell, the pit, as they called it, wasn't a place anyone planned on going. It wasn't a career path you chose. But once you were there, once you'd made the deals necessary to claw your way into a position with even a shred of power, you did what was required to stay out of there.

"Let's just concentrate on the human," he said, refusing to engage with her questions. Refusing to acknowledge the uncomfortable truth buried in them.

"I already am concentrating on him." Gabriella's attention shifted back to Colin, and her expression softened into something almost tender. "He's quite handsome, isn't he? Those honey-colored eyes, that smile. If I were human, I think one look would melt my heart."

"Women on earth know better than to fall for him," Devon countered. "They see through the charm to the emptiness underneath. I could have this case wrapped up before Christmas if you'd just stay out of my way."

"Too bad." Gabriella's smile was pure determination. "I'm here to keep you from destroying him. I'm sure you have all sorts of nasty temptations planned, money, power, all the things that speak to his worst instincts. But with my guidance, he'll find something worth changing for. Something worth being better for."

Devon studied her, this infuriating angel with her leather outfit and her unwavering faith in human nature. She still believed she could save everyone. Still believed love and redemption could triumph over darkness.

It would almost be admirable if it wasn't so naive.

"No," he said firmly, turning his full attention back to Colin McDermott, who was now laughing with his colleagues, completely unaware that his immortal soul had become a battleground. "By Christmas, he'll be mine. Count on it."

"We'll see." Gabriella's voice held a note of steel beneath the sweetness. "I've never backed down from a challenge before, Devon. I'm not starting now."

They stood there in silence for a moment, two ancient beings watching one oblivious human, each determined to pull him in opposite directions. The eternal struggle between damnation and salvation, playing out in the heart of a man who had no idea he was about to become ground zero in a cosmic battle.

Devon smiled grimly. This was going to be interesting.

And he was absolutely going to win.

The Reluctant Santa
Available Everywhere

Return to Cupid Box Set Books 7-9
Return to Cupid Box Set Books 10-12
**The Unlucky Bride

Contemporary Romance
My Sister's Boyfriend
The Wanted Bride
The Reluctant Santa
The Relationship Coach
Secrets, Lies, & Online Dating

Bride, Texas Multi-Author Series
**The Unlucky Bride

Coming Home for Christmas
I'll Be Home for Christmas
White Christmas
Santa's Baby
All I Want For Christmas

Lipstick and Lead 2.0
Nailing the Hit Man
Nailing the Billionaire
Nailing the Single Dad

Secrets of Mustang Island
Secrets of a Summer Place
Secrets of a Runaway Bride
Secrets From the Past

The Langley Legacy
Collin's Challenge

Short Sexy Reads
Racy Reunions Series
Paying For the Past
My Christmas Soldier
Cupid's Revenge

Western Historicals
A Hero's Heart
Second Chance Cowboy
Ethan

American Brides
**Katie: Bride of Virginia

Angel Creek Christmas Brides
**Charity
**Ginger
**Minne
**Cora
Angel Creek Christmas Box Set

Bad Girls of the West
Scandalous Sadie
Ravenous Rose
Tempting Tessa
Nellie's Redemption

The Burnett Brides Series
The Rancher Takes A Bride
The Outlaw Takes A Bride
The Marshal Takes A Bride
The Christmas Bride
Boxed Set

Lipstick and Lead Series
Desperate
Deadly
Dangerous
Daring
**Determined
Deceived
Defiant
Devious
Lipstick and Lead Box Set Books 1-4
Lipstick and Lead Box Set Books 5-9
Lipstick and Lead Box Set Books 1-9
**Quinlan's Quest

Mail Order Bride Tales
**A Brother's Betrayal
**Pearl
**Ace's Bride

Scandalous Suffragettes of the West
**Abigail
Bella

Mistletoe Scandal

Southern Historical Romance
A Scarlet Bride

The Cuvier Women
Wronged
Betrayed
Beguiled
Boxed Set

The Debutante's of Durango
The Debutante's Scandal
The Debutante's Gamble
The Debutante's Revenge
The Debutante's Santa
Box Set

**** Denotes a sweet book.**

Want to learn about my new releases before anyone else? Sign up for my New Book Alert and receive a complimentary book.

USA Today Best-selling author, Sylvia McDaniel obviously has too much time on her hands. With over ninety western historical and contemporary romance novels, she spends most days torturing her characters. Bad boys deserve punishment and even good girls get into trouble. Always looking for the next plot twist, she's known for her sweet, funny, family-oriented romances.

Married to her best friend for over twenty-five years, they recently moved to the state of Colorado where they like to hike, and enjoy the beauty of the forest behind their home with their spoiled dachshund Zeus. (He has his own column in her newsletter.)

Their grown son, still lives in Texas. An avid football watcher, she loves the Broncos and the Cowboys, especially when they're winning.

www.SylviaMcDaniel.com
The End